TRIANGLES

OF

DECEPTION

Renee Robinson

Triangles of Deception

Renee Robinson

Triangles of Deception   Renee Robinson

Bulk quantities are available for distribution. Please contact R&R
Publishing, LLC, P.O. Box 25962, Richmond, VA 23260.
Telephone: 804-537-0211

ISBN: 978-0-9973588-0-3

Triangles of Deception   Renee Robinson

Acknowledgements

First and foremost, I would like to thank God for speaking to me in writing this book. I feel like with God in your life all things are possible. I kept telling my husband and friends that I wanted to write a book, and guess what… I did! I would like to thank my husband for staying up long nights and listening to me relentlessly go on about this book, for being a listening ear and giving feedback. I want to thank all my friends for being there and listening to me about this book. It is truly a lot of you guys to name. It means a lot to me that I have you guys support. I haven't forgot about any of you, you know who you are. To my children I love you! Canaan we did it! Thank you so much, I definitely couldn't have done this without you! This is my first book, so I hope you enjoy it as much as I did writing it.

This book focuses on the marriage life, friendship, betrayal, broken trust, ignorance, and selfishness. Marriage takes work and a lot of it. It also brings up issues on mental health and awareness. Mental illness is just like a physical illness. Just because you do not see it doesn't mean it's not there.

Enjoy!

Triangles of Deception   Renee Robinson

Prologue

I hear beeping noises; the voices are muffled…. I can barely breathe….my head hurts….I can't move…. my body feels like it has been hit by a Mack truck. I hear voices say, "we are losing her." I hear more beeping and then it begins beeping faster. I closed my eyes…. I'm too weak to fight. I tried to speak…. but my throat is dry…. I tried to scream, but I can't get the words out. What happened? As I lay here, I reflected on my life and ask myself, how did I get here? Where did I go wrong? Where did we go wrong? I had it…. I had the perfect life…. the perfect husband…. I was the perfect wife…. I had it all. I heard two voices going back and forth.

"What are you doing here?"

"What do you mean what am I doing here, what are you doing here?"

I was drifting in and out of consciousness, so I could only hear bits and pieces of the conversation.

"This is not the time nor place."

"What do you mean?"

Am I dead? People stopped talking.

Another voice enters the room. I heard her say,

"We aren't sure of her condition, and she is currently in a coma. We do not know if she will make it as the next few hours are critical. She is not alert to her surroundings. We are just waiting over the next 24 hours to reevaluate her condition."

Then I drifted off again. I don't know what in store for me. But I'm definitely going to make a change if I survive this. Now I'm lying here asking myself where did I go wrong. I went wrong everywhere and let me tell you why.

Shawna

I was celebrating my 25th birthday with my girlfriends and this idiot bumps into me almost breaking my shoulder off.

"Excuse you!"

"My bad ma. I apologize you aight?"

"Yea, I'm good, next time watch where you're going!" I had an attitude.

"Yo! I said my bad! What you want me to do?"

When I got a good look at him, I realized this man was fine as hell. He was about 6'3, 220, chocolate complexion, hazel brown eyes, muscular build. Maybe I shouldn't have such a bad attitude. I immediately became shy.

"It's ok." I began to walk off, when he spoke up.

"Yo, me and my boys going up into this club. what are you and your girls doing tonight? Y'all want to roll?"

"It's my birthday, I am turning 25 tonight so I'm definitely trying to turn up tonight."

"I didn't get ya name ma. I'm Terrance by the way but everybody calls me T-Money."

"Well, I'm Shawna, nice to meet you Terrance."

The whole night Terrance and I danced together. It was like we were inseparable. He asked for my number and I didn't hesitate to give it to him. Terrance asked me to go home with him that night. I wasn't going to go home with someone I didn't know. My best friend Lisa hooked up with one of his boys, I told her to go ahead without me. She seemed like she had fun.

Three weeks went by and I hadn't heard from him. I was sitting at my desk remembering how fine this man was. He appeared to be a drug dealer or something, especially the way he was dressed. He probably got a whole flock of women chasing him. Damn, Shawna you should have gotten his number. My receptionist beeps in and says my 3:00 meeting is in the conference room. Great, now I can talk to this investment banker and listen to them try to market some strategies to partner with our firm. When I walked into the conference room, I almost had a heart attack. It was him, it was T-Money aka Terrance, except this time he wasn't dressed like he was in the streets. He looked like something out of Forbes magazine.

"Hello…. Mr. James, I'm Ms. Taylor it's nice to meet you." I was mean mugging him.

I tried to keep it professional, but the inside of me was just screaming, he's here! Truth is, I didn't want him to know that I was excited to see him so I gave him the cold shoulder.

"Hello Ms. Taylor, it's finally nice to meet you again."

I saw Mr. Johnson give me the side eye. I knew I would have to explain later. After sitting talking marketing strategies with his investment firm for nearly two hours. I expressed that I would have to get back with him and speak to my partner about joining their firm. As he was about to walk out the door, he turned around.

"Ms. Taylor, here is my card. I look forward to hearing from you. Oh and I apologize for losing yours." He winked.

I took his number without cracking a smile.

"We will be in touch."

I turn and Mr. Johnson is giving me the evil eye.

"What's that look for?"

"Who is he Shawna?"

"Nobody."

"Nobody…. huh? He sure wasn't looking at you like you were a nobody."

He kept staring at me, like he was staring hole in me.

"Ok! I met him a few weeks ago. I had no idea he was in the financial industry. You know my birthday was a few weeks ago. I went to a club and we met. I gave him my number he never called, case closed."

"Ok Shawna, don't let his man make a fool of you twice. You hear me?"

"Ok, Mr. Johnson."

Mr. Johnson was like the fatherly figure I needed sometimes. I wanted to call him, I felt like I had to. He said he lost my number. Was it true? Why did he have to be so charming? I went back to my office and toyed around with the idea of calling him. Lisa entered my office. Lisa and I have been friends since high school. When I made it to the financial world, I gave her a job as my receptionist.

"Hey Lisa, what's up?"

"Was that the guy from the club?"

"Yea.... that was him."

"He looked totally different from when we saw him."

"Yeah, same thing I said, turns out he is a co-owner of this firm across the street. He wants to partner with us."

"Oh yea.... I mean if the numbers look good I say go for it."

"I haven't really reviewed the numbers yet. He slid me his number Lisa. I don't know if I want to call him or not."

"Girl! You better call that man! When was the last time you have been out on a date anyway?"

"You're right, I just don't want to mix business with pleasure.... you know."

"Then don't. Y'all are going out on a date. Don't go home with him, or even let him kiss you until you have reviewed those numbers. That way it won't cloud your judgment."

"I guess." I was apprehensive.

"Alright girl, let me get back to my desk, the phone has been ringing all day."

Lisa has always given me the most honest advice when it came to men. Sometimes I have taken her advice, sometimes I haven't. What do I have to lose by calling him? Lisa hooked up with one of his friends from the club and went home with him that night. They were still talking she said.

I was so nervous about calling Terrance that I dialed his number 5 times and hung up. Finally, I got the courage to speak.

"Hello, may I speak to Terrance?" I heard a laugh.

"Who else would it be if I gave you my number?"

"I don't know." I laughed nervously. I can't believe I'm actually talking to him. Why did I feel like a groupie?

"How are you doing Ms. Taylor?"

"I'm doing ok, just getting comfortable at home."

"Why are you doing that? I am supposed to be taking you out on a date tonight. Can you be ready by 9:00? Meet me at the Italian Restaurant on Main Street."

"See you there."

I scrambled around trying to figure out what to wear that night. I'll keep it light and wear my cherry red and white Christian Louboutins, with my red and white strapless dress. I take one last look at myself in the mirror before I step out. Terrance was there before I was looking like a million bucks.

"Damn, baby you look fine as hell." Terrance was admiring my dress.

A few drinks later I realized that Terrance and I had a lot in common. We were both young, black and successful. We both didn't have any kids, and didn't want any anytime soon, unless we were married. I realized he began young in the financial field just like I did. But it was something about him that just didn't fit. It was like he was a Wall Street thug. No matter how much he dressed it up, it seemed like his come up was in the streets. He had a swagger. He talked professional in the meeting, but every now and then he would get too comfortable and some "hood" would come out. I should have known that by the way he was dressed in the club though. I brushed it off as him growing up with a hard life. Terrance says he never had anything easy. His mother had 5 children and he never knew his father. His mother worked a lot to provide but it was better than nothing. He said his mother died a few years ago, and has little contact with his siblings. Terrance and I talked for hours. It just seemed like we clicked. Terrance walked me to my car. He was such a gentleman.

"Is this your idea of buttering me up? So we can partner with you?"

"Is it working?"

"Maybe."

Everything seemed so perfect in the moment. I knew I couldn't let this cloud my judgment. He leaned in to kiss me,

"Ah ah," as I waved my finger teasing him. We have business. I will be in touch Mr. James."

The next morning, I reviewed all the numbers. The numbers looked good. Almost too good to good to be true. I called Mr. Johnson in to make sure we were looking at everything right. They were a smaller company looking to partner with a bigger firm. We weren't totally against it. But we had to make sure things were in our favor.

"What do you think Mr. Johnson?"

"They look amazing, Shawna. But I have to admit it's something about that Terrance guy."

"What do you mean?"

"His personality. He is a charmer. A sweet talker. I noticed his main focus was on you."

"This is business, Mr. Johnson. As long as the numbers look good, I don't care how he was looking at me."

"Ok Shawna, it's your call."

I reflected on everything that Mr. Johnson was saying. Mr. Johnson was like a mentor to me and also a fatherly figure since my father died. I always took his advice seriously. He was right, it was something about him. I didn't want last night to cloud my judgment, but our date was amazing. I looked down at my phone and noticed that Terrance texted me:

"Hey babe I enjoyed last night. I can't wait to do it again."

I looked at the message, but I didn't respond. C'mon Shawna get your head out of the clouds. I wasn't always good at picking out the right men. But he seemed to have it together. Successful, no kids, and a business man nonetheless. I think I am going to go ahead and accept the deal. What did we have to lose? The numbers look good.

After accepting the deal, things took off with Terrance and I. We went on dates, a lot of them. We were able to keep our lives separate from the office. The office was business.

We got married, had a kid, the rest is history.

****

Eight years later here we are with a son in tow. Terrance is so good to me. He has been an amazing provider for me and our son. I never thought anything out of the ordinary about Terrance, because he always did what he was supposed to as a man. I must admit these eight years haven't been the easiest. Early in our marriage, I thought we were going to divorce because of my depression, but we worked things out. Terrance has always like to control the finances which was ok with me, because that was all I dealt with at work were numbers. When he wanted to take over, I wasn't totally against it. Terrance waltzes in after work.

"Hey babe, what are we having for dinner?"

It is always his favorite. I can read his mind before he says it.

"It smells like my favorite, spaghetti?"

"And you know it."

He is so predictable, routine people may even call him. Terrance is the model husband, he works a 9-5 every day and comes home to me and our son TJ. He occasionally goes to the gym after work. I am a stay at home mom. Terrance has always wanted me to stay at home after I had our son. The biggest issue was that I wasn't built to be a stay at home mom, I knew nothing about babies. Luckily, I had my mom. That only went so far until I started pushing everyone away. Terrance almost forced me to stay at home, but I wanted to still keep up with the day to day finances with the company. However, over time I began keeping up less and I guess he noticed.

"Baby, are you there?" Terrance says, as he snaps me out of my thoughts.

"What are you thinking about?"

"Nothing, honey just how happy I am with you and TJ."

"I love you baby you mean the world to me."

"Mommy, mommy, can I have a snack before dinner?" TJ asks.

"No! You cannot have a snack before dinner, maybe after dinner."

"Pleaaaaaasssssseeeeee." TJ whines.

"No, dinner will be ready in a few."

TJ looks just like his father only with my complexion, but TJ has all his father's physical characteristics. Terrance has always wanted TJ to go to the best schools since he grew up in the streets of Baltimore. I must admit for a 7-year-old, TJ is pretty witty. His scholarly education has really paid off so far.

After dinner is served, I looked over to my husband who seems to always be happy. I wish I could feel the same. Yes, I have the husband, the child, the house, the cars, and I must say we are very well off, others may even call us "rich." Something is missing, it's always missing. It's the same thing every night. He may be a great provider, but he is lacking in the sex department. He is a selfish lover, and always finishes first. Maybe that's why we almost divorced, or was it that he had his controlling moments. He doesn't like to do oral sex, but always wants me to suck his dick. Excuse my language but that's how it is. He doesn't care about my needs at all. I'm trying to figure out now how to get out of having sex with him tonight, a headache? Diarrhea? Tired? Terrance won't go for any of it because he figures I stay at home, and do nothing all day and the least I could do is have sex with him. att least that what he says. I suggest something new, he doesn't want to do it. I wonder how did we get to this point; sex wasn't always this way.

"Shawna. Shawna, earth to Shawna? You there? You are always zoning out? You ok?"

"Yea I'm ok, I was just thinking."

Most women would die for the life I have, but what most women fail to understand is that I had my own before I got married. We were a power couple together, and when we got married that's when things went downhill. Within the first 3 months I was pregnant with my son, I stepped down at the company and became a stay at home mom. He took over the company. I just thought things would be better than this, maybe I don't know that man I married.

Terrance

My life wasn't always the greatest. My brother and I are the oldest of 5 kids, we're twins. His name is Terrell, he was the smart one. He didn't end up in the streets like I did. My mom did the best she could to provide for us, but her best just wasn't good enough. I am not saying it to sound harsh. But I wanted what the other kids had and that's how I ended up in the dope game. She died a month after me and Terrell turned 18. She always said I would be the death of her. I wonder if it's true sometimes. They said it was a heart attack. Shortly after that, we both finished high school. Terrell went off to college and never looked back. But I stayed back to make sure my sister's and youngest brother were ok. I didn't want them going into foster care or nothing, so I took care of them. I had two sisters Talyah, and Tamia and my baby brother Daron. All of us were about a year apart. It was hard keeping everyone on track, because I didn't want them to live the lifestyle I did. Both of my sisters did end up going to college. But my baby brother wanted to be in the game like I did. No matter how much I tried to steer him away from it, and encouraged him to be like Terrell. He just was attracted to the game. Instead of Daron going to work for some other street thug, I had him working for me doing stuff like picking up money, something I hoped he wouldn't end up dead. But as luck would have it, Daron ended up getting killed a year or so into the game by some knuckleheads that were trying to rob me. My family blamed me for Daron's death. Hell, I blamed myself, so needless to say I don't maintain contact with any of my family anymore. They disowned me after the funeral. They made it very clear not to contact them anymore. So I didn't. When I got married and had a kid, no one knew.

I had been in the dope game since I was 15, I started off little, but I came up quick. I had shit on lock in Maryland. Now I'm 26 years old, I knew I had to do something different. I got tired of running, and looking over my back. I wanted to get out. Lucky for me I never been locked up either. The main reason I knew I had to get out of the game, because I knew I would either end up dead or locked up. I knew some things needed to change.

That night I was out celebrating when I met Shawna. Me and my boy Brian had got our investment firm up and running. I didn't have a college education like Brian did, but I knew my shit inside and out. Brian was the front runner, because he had the education. But I had the money, so together I felt like we were unstoppable. The money we had coming in was clean, and nobody could take that from us. I felt relaxed and ready to turn up.

I met Shawna a few years back. Damn it seemed like a lifetime ago at a club. I was celebrating with a few of my boys. I bumped into her, I have to admit I was a little disrespectful. I had some drinks in me. I stepped back and she had it going on. Truth is that night I was just trying to fuck. I wasn't trying to call her. When she didn't go home with me that night, I was like fuck it and tossed her number. I had just gotten out a tight relationship with my ex, so the last thing I wanted to do is try to get serious with some hoe in the club.

A few weeks went by Shawna never even crossed my mind. I was at work reflecting on business. All we needed was this firm to partner with us, and it's a done deal. I had a meeting with Ms. Taylor, and Mr. Johnson, their firm was right across the street from ours. We were small, but we were building. When Ms. Taylor walked in I almost shitted on myself. Damn, why didn't I call her? Shit the way she was dressed I didn't think she ran this bitch. It was this older black guy in there too. How am I going to get myself out of this one.

"Hello Mr. James, I'm Ms. Taylor."

She was mean mugging me. I didn't know what to think. If I wasn't on some other shit, I could have gotten to know her played my cards right, and we would have been in there. I was nervous as shit, because I just knew I had fucked up this one. She never cracked a smile, or even looked my way, at the end of the meeting she said she would be in touch. I tried my luck.

"Here is my card, Ms. Taylor, I look forward to hearing from you soon." I winked. She didn't even crack a smile.

"Thank You, Mr. James we will be in touch."

I went back to the office telling Brian how I think I fucked up. Brian was with us that night, and he remembered Shawna and her friend Lisa all to well. Brian hooked up with Lisa that night, I just went home with a hard dick.

"Man…. she might not even remember you Terrance."

"Oh, she remembered me, she mean mugged me the entire meeting."

"I slid her my number on the low though. I hope she call."

"She won't call."

"If she calls man that's our way in. Damn, I hope she calls."

That evening Shawna called. I thought it was my ex playing games because the phone would ring before a number showed up. I was with another chick I was just fucking when Shawna called. I had to think quick. I offered to take her to dinner that night, and the rest was history.

We moved kind of fast. Shawna was about her business, and I knew how to get to her was through her heart. We went on a lot of dates, things got serious fast. I was really feeling her to the point I cut off all the women I talked to. I proposed and now here we are.

****

My wife sure knew how to piss me off, I try not to upset her. But she is sensitive these days. Sometimes it's like she zones out or something I must admit I have changed over the years, but she has too. I treat her how a Queen deserves to be treated. But I swear my wife think she knows me. She has no idea. I don't know if she cooks the same thing every day to piss me off, or she really does think I'm that predictable. I volunteer to cook or take her and TJ out to eat. She refuses and then suggests that we should save money. She doesn't realize how much money we have, I keep her away from the finances. I can't have her trying to run off with all my money. Don't get me wrong, she came into the marriage with a townhome, car and assets of her own. But I had more, I was pretty sure I had more. We rented out her townhouse, and she kept her car, but I was trying to convince her to merge assets. I'll give her that she is very intelligent, which was part of the reason I married her. I do control the finances, assets, and anything that has to do with money. She has an allowance she can shop with each month, which is more than enough. Truth is I don't want her to work because then she would be 50/50 in my company. I'm not saying I don't trust her, but where I'm from we protect ourselves first.

Shawna is 5'5 light skin complexion with dark brown chestnut eyes. Her eyes are slanted, and her hair is wavy which comes to the middle of her back. My wife, yea she is fine. I must admit is another reason I had to snatch her up. We had our son TJ who looks just like me. She told me she didn't want any kids, but had TJ for me. I got her pregnant on purpose. I even tried to get her pregnant a few more times. It wasn't meant to be or she had to be on birth control because it never happened. I made her think that we mutually agreed to it. To this day, I still think she resents the idea. I admit Shawna gave me a run for my money, it was hard to lock her down. It was well worth it. Our marriage has been strained these days. Sex is always an issue. She always has a headache, toothache, her stomach hurts, her feet hurts, something is always hurting. The least she can do is fuck me every once in a while. She is always whining. Can we do this? Can we do that? It might sound selfish but most of the time it's a no. We tried it her way and I didn't like it. Truth is our sex life changed when TJ was born. Shawna was a straight freak. We had sex everywhere and couldn't get enough of each other. We fucked so much, I knew I had a keeper. But once TJ was born, well she resented it and me. Everything went downhill. No more sex, no more freaky sex, no more head just no more anything. All she do is complain. I want the old Shawna back. I tell her she has changed since TJ but she doesn't want to hear it. She says I changed, HA! Can you believe that shit? I know she isn't going to want to fuck tonight so I might as well hit the gym tonight after dinner and release the extra stress.

"Hey baby, I'm going to hit the gym tonight. You look like you don't feel well."

"Ok that's fine honey. See you later."

That was easy, I jumped in my Chevrolet Silverado. I kept wondering how did me and Shawna get to where we are? We've been together for eight years now and this is where we are at. Don't get me wrong, I love my wife but I don't get what I need from my wife. I keep her away from the things she doesn't need to know. Honestly, it's none of her concern. I've had my share of infidelities over the years but I still take care of home. I ain't one of those bum dudes that's out here cheating and ain't taking care of home.

I walked into the gym, usually it the same ole same ole people. It wasn't that packed, I spot a few people that I might be interested in. I climb on the treadmill and I peeped the person next to me.

"Hey, how are you?"

"I'm good." I do a once over. Not bad.

"Nice night for a workout. You from around here?"

Why they asking so many questions? Let me be nice. I do want some ass tonight.

"Nah I'm not from around here." I lied.

"Ok, I'm Jamie by the way."

"Nice to meet you Jamie. My name is Terrance."

Things got quiet. I noticed Jamie checking me out. I noticed that Jamie wasn't bad looking. The gym is where all the single people hang out to try to snag a man, or fuck one. I'm ok with either one. I try to switch up gym's, because you just never know who's lurking around. Jamie continues talking.

"How long have you been coming to this gym?"

"For about a month now."

"I am new here. I just found this gym. It's a pretty nice gym I think."

I admit I get shy when I talk to new people although I talk to new people every day at work. In my personal life it's different. I can't explain how it's different, it just is. I know I look good as hell. Who wouldn't want me? After I get a good look, I realized that Jamie is fine as hell. Jamie is about 5'9 caramel complexion, curly hair, green eyes, and the most beautiful legs I've ever seen in my life, and that ass DAMN! Come on, Terrance snap out of it, you haven't been here 5 minutes and you already got some new booty.

"Well, Terrance it's nice to meet you. I hope to see you around some time."

"Wait, here is my number call me some time." I take one last look at Jamie. Damn I can't wait to get up in that.

I finally get home my wife is sleep of course. She always asleep. I think she be faking it sometimes, so I won't mess with her. Damn that Jamie was fine as hell.

Shawna

Terrance gets in the bed. I pretend I'm sleep, no need in him thinking I'm woke and want to fuck tonight. He kisses me on my forehead and hops in the shower. I'm glad I trust him. I know women be all over him at the gym. I hear the shower running, and I doze off to sleep. It's 6:30 a.m. and my alarm is ringing in my ear. It lets me know that it's time to get TJ up for school. I rolled over, Terrance is still asleep. I try to slide out of bed, but not before Terrance catches me.

"Come on baby, one for the road before you get TJ up."

"I can't Terrance, you know TJ can't be late for school! You know how strict the schedule is at the school you wanted him to go to!"

Terrance mumbles something. It must have just been a bad morning because I snap back and ask him.

"What did you just say?"

I rarely talked back to Terrance because he is known to have a bit of a temper. I was tired of him treating me like a 1950's housewife, like I'm supposed to be at his every beck and call. Terrance snatches the cover off, gets out the bed and gets in my face.

"I said, here you go with this shit again, is it too much to ask for my wife to suck my dick?" He was so close to me, I could feel the spit hit my face while he was talking.

I rolled my eyes and begin to walk away. I wanted to tell
him it is! It really is. Terrance has never laid a hand on me,
but he has gotten in my face a few times.

"TJ, honey it's time to wake up for school, TJ, wake up."
As I continued to shake him.

"Mommy, do I have to?"

"Yes you do, school is the most important thing you will
ever do in life."

"Well, mommy I don't want to go. The kids make fun of
me because I'm black, they say I don't belong there."

"Oh honey, don't believe what they say you are smarter
than they are. That is why they are mad. Mommy will come
to the school today and talk to the Principal, ok?"

"Ok…. mommy, is daddy coming too?"

"I don't know, but I will see."

Terrance has a presence about him that could intimidate
anyone. Which was probably why TJ asked. I resented the
idea of children, but now that TJ is here, he is my world. I
think Terrance still thinks I resent the idea. I'm not saying
that I wasn't a bitch when TJ was born, but I was
miserable, my feet were swollen, I was big as a house,
stretch marks and I couldn't keep anything down. I blamed
Terrance the entire pregnancy All Terrance talked about
while I was pregnant was having more kids.. Afterwards I
felt like he made me stay at home with TJ and I knew
nothing about babies. I was raised as an only child even

though I had an older sister that was ten years older. My experience with small children, especially babies was limited. I looked at TJ and wonder how I could ever resent him, I love him.

"Mommy, mommy, can you help me? I'm stuck."

I laughed as I watch TJ struggles to get his head through his shirt.

"Finish getting dressed for school, and meet me downstairs for breakfast."

I walked downstairs reflecting on the incident that happened earlier. I wondered would I marriage improve. I cooked breakfast for TJ and myself. Fuck him, he can make his own breakfast. I didn't complete my entire thought until Terrance snuck up behind me.

"I'm sorry baby, can you forgive me?"

"This is not a conversation I want to have right now, when TJ is on his way downstairs. Can you go to school with me today? I quickly changed the subject. TJ says that other kids are teasing him because he is black and saying that he doesn't belong there."

"What? Ah hell no, I pay good money for TJ to go there every month! I'll be damned if TJ is dealing with some white racist kids! I'm going to hop in the shower, and I'll go with you!"

****

"Hello, how may I help you?" The receptionist asks.

"Hi, my husband and I are here to see the Principal. It's very urgent that we speak with him."

"Can I get your names please?"

"Shawna James and Terrance James."

"Please have a seat and he will be right with you."

This older white man walks out and greets the both of us.

"Hi, Mr. and Mrs. James how are you today. What brings you to my office this morning?"

"Well…. we aren't doing so well." Terrance spoke up first.

"My son says that he is being bullied at your school, and I pay good money for my son to be here at your school. He reports that he is being called a nigger, and he doesn't belong at this school. Now Mr. Toler, I don't appreciate the racism that is going on with your school especially at such a young age. I believe we can work to resolve this."

I don't remember telling Terrance saying that the kids called him a nigger.

"Mr. James I apologize that your son is being bullied. But you know how kids are at this age. They tease those that are different from them. I am unsure of what you would like me to do about it."

I immediately notice the grimace on Terrance's face as if he was about to explode. I began to rub his leg to remind him of where we are, and to calm his temper.

"Mr. Toler, if you don't mind me asking how many children of different races do you have at your school? I mean African-American, Hispanic, Korean or Chinese?"

"I'm unsure, Mr. James we have a lot of children so it's hard to keep up."

"Mr. Toler I can tell you that my son Terrance James Jr. is the second black child in your school. If you don't do something about it, I will go to your school board and complain until someone does. Not only does my son go to school here, I donate a lot of money to this school."

"Well… Mr. James so do the other parents."

I hate that Terrance flashes his money around, like money can buy everything. I must admit he does have a lot of pull at the school.

"Mr. James, we will see what we can do. I'll get back with you by the end of the day."

We walked out of the office. Terrance still seemed pissed off. I didn't know if it was a good time to talk to him right at this moment. I didn't think it could wait.

"Honey, are you going to work today?"

"No, I gotta run a few errands, but I will be back home."

"Can we talk when you get back?"

"I have some time now, talk."

"Well, um." I immediately begin to stutter, because I didn't know how Terrance would respond to my next statement.

"Come on, Shawna spit it out, what do you want to talk about?"

"I want to go back to work Terrance, TJ is 7 years old, I miss working. I'm not saying I don't enjoy being a stay at home mom. But I do miss working. I talked to Mr. Johnson a week ago, and he says I can begin work next week. I feel like that is the part of me that I'm missing." I felt like I was rambling.

"Baby if that's what you want to do, go ahead."

That wasn't the response that I was expecting from Terrance. I expected him to be mad or upset but he wasn't, he was supportive. God, I love this man. We might have our ups and down. I must say that he has been nothing but the perfect husband to me. He deserves more from me. He deserves his wife back and maybe going back to work is the motivation that I need to feel fulfilled.

Terrance

I don't know what the hell Shawna's problem was this morning, but she definitely pissed me off this morning. All of that shit was uncalled for. All I wanted was some head, and she couldn't even give me that. But its cool though. This is why I do the shit I do. Shawna tries she does, but her best isn't good enough. Now before you go judging me, Shawna never could cook, and I cook sometimes. But she wanted to learn, so she went out and brought all these cook books, I was always supportive in everything she wanted to do. But she still couldn't cook. Poor TJ, cereal and waffles every morning is what she gives him. Pitiful.

I apologized to Shawna because she didn't deserve how I snapped on her this morning. But I immediately got pissed off again because she told me TJ was getting picked on a school but some little white racist kids. It's a fucking shame that it still exists. I donate a lot of money to that fucking school so that last thing they want to do is piss me off. I don't give a fuck about anybody else in that school, I only care about my son. Mr. Toler acted like he didn't know me, because of my wife sitting there. But me and Mr. Toler go way back before he was Principal. Ask him who got him his job as Principal. Now it's his fucking job to make sure my son doesn't get picked on. He can expel the little fuckers for all I care, as long as my son is good. He knows what's up. Shawna sits there as if she is clueless, she hates the fact that we have a lot of money. She is frugal, humble even, but shit who said money couldn't buy things.

Now when Shawna told me she wanted to go back to work, I was like damn could this day get any fucking worse. I wanted to be supportive of Shawna, but I know if Shawna goes back to work I'm a liability. I don't know if you've peeped this yet, but Shawna was the CEO of the investment firm that my company is a partner with. But when the owner of the company got sick, I think with cancer or something. He left Shawna the company. But my company S&A Investment firm, I own 25% of S&A, and 25% of A&M, which only leaves me owning less than 50% of each company. Now if Shawna comes back, Shawna will own 50% of the company. But her 50% is only reinstated if she comes back to work, so right now I own 75% of the company. I am authorized to act as CEO in her absence. I want my partner to sell his share so I can have 100% ownership of the company. But he is refusing so I'll settle for the 75%. So as you can see, I don't want her back to work, because then she will be my boss calling all the shots again. I can't afford that, but if she wants to come back to work. I'll let her, but she will quickly realize how things have changed since she has been gone. She may not want to but she will be answering to me, not vice versa. My phone goes off in the middle of Shawna talking to me.

I look down at my phone, and receive a text from Tonya:

"Hey boo, wyd, you coming through later?"

I text her back:

"nah not today."

Tonya was this chick I met at her job way back when I was trying to partner with her firm. She was the receptionist. She isn't clingy or nothing but she is old news now. She been around for a minute now, about five years. She knows about my wife; I pay her to keep quiet. Truth is I was ready to leave Shawna for her, but something wasn't right about her. But I ain't fucked with her in about two weeks or so now, so that's only going to go so long. I'm going to get rid of her. But I need to make sure she is definitely long gone before I give her the boot. I get another text; I step out the room with Shawna after congratulating her on wanting to return to work. It's from Dana. Dana and I been messing with for about two years now. I met Dana at one of those PTA meetings when Shawna couldn't go. I might need to go hit Dana up, I could sure use some head right now. I told Shawna I need to run some errands. Dana texts:

"Hey baby I sure need you inside me right now."
I reply:

"Be there in an hour."

I kiss Shawna on the cheek and tell her I'll be back by the time TJ gets home. Dana was a straight freak, and I loved it! I think its what I was missing in my life. I get to Dana's house. Dana is pretty decent looking, not ugly by far. Dana is 5'7, a little lighter than I am, dark brown eyes, slim and thick in all the right places, and that ass, I can't wait to tear that ass up.

"Hey baby, I missed you."

"Hmmph, hmph I missed you too."

Dana immediately pulls my dick out and starts sucking it. I thought I was about to cum in the first 2 minutes. Damn, this shit is overdue. I tell Dana get up, let me hit it from behind.

"Ok baby, you know how I like it."

I spread that ass wide and go in slow, damn it's so tight. Why can't Shawna fuck me more often were the thoughts going through my mind. I start fucking Dana harder and faster. Dana starts throwing that ass back and playing with my balls. Damn that shit feels so good.

"You gon' let me cum all over the ass baby."

"Oh yessssss baby, cum all over this ass."

I feel it coming, and I begin to explode. Dana turns around and begins sucking the cum off my dick, damn I love some head. I pull my pants up, and get ready to go.

"Look baby, I gotta go I'll see you later."

"Damn, Terrance you always gotta go. Am I just a piece of ass for you?"

"Nah, you know you not. Come on don't act like that. I'll catch up with you later."

Dana leans in to try to kiss me, I turn my cheek. I never kiss these hoes in the mouth. Rule #1.

Jamie

He walked into the gym looking like something out of GQ magazine. I immediately observed him, and he was definitely my type. I saw him get on the treadmill, so did I. I try to make small talk.

"It's a beautiful night tonight, don't you think?"

"Yea."

"My name is Jamie by the way."

"What's up my name is Terrance."

Even though he wasn't trying to I noticed him checking me out. I thought I wouldn't be his type, but I guess I am He was a bit more standoffish than I expected, but that is to be expected from a man like him. I pretended to drop something so I can bend over in front him so I could be sure he was looking at me and BAM! He was looking at my ass like he wanted to eat it for dinner. So I made my move, men like him figures he can get anyone he wants. So I gotta make him chase it.

"Well, Terrance it was nice to meet you, hope to see you around sometime."

"Yo, wait here is my number call me some time."

I didn't want him to think I was thirsty so I would wait a few days before would call him, because I know he is expecting my call.

The next day, I go into work and the receptionist says Jamie you have a call on Line 1. These damn pricks early in the morning, what do they want. I haven't even had coffee yet.

"Heeey Jamie, oh shit it's my mother."

"Hi mom."

"How are you Jamie?"

"I'm good mom, what's going on?"

"Nothing I wanted to check on you, make sure everything is ok. We are having a family function in a few weeks, I wanted to see if you wanted to come."

"Sure mom…. I'll be there."

"Oh good, see you there." Uuughh my mom can be such a nuisance, but she is sweet as pie. Well, if anything its good food, and good entertainment. I hadn't seen my mom in a very long time so I know she is looking forward to me being there.

I sit at my desk looking at the number in my phone wondering should I text or call today. Nah I'll wait another day; I don't want Terrance to think I'm on his dick like that even though I want the dick. I could definitely tell he was packing it was showing through his shorts.

"Jamie, you have a call on Line 2." My receptionist says.

My receptionist interrupted my thoughts. It was Mr. Johnson, so she is on board, great, I can't wait to meet her, meeting next Monday at 9:00 right?

Shawna

I arrived to work early. Terrance offered to take TJ to school. My first meeting was at 9:00 a.m. with a Jamie Mitchell. We were going to review some investment portfolios. My first day at work was no walk in the park. Terrance could have told me things have changed. We don't work in the same building, but I could definitely see the dynamics have changed. My office was the same way I left it. This was going to be a long day.

"Mrs. James, Jamie is in Conference Room 1."

"Thank you, Lisa."

I walked towards the conference room. I didn't know why I felt so nervous about this meeting.

"How are you doing, Mrs. James? "

"Please call me Shawna."

"Well, Shawna, how are you doing, I'm Jamie, nice to meet you."

"Well let's talk business. I know I've been gone awhile, but I'm still the same person."

"That's what Mr. Johnson tells me. He says you're the best. Is it true that you and your husband own the company together?"

"We do.... I have decided to return to work since our son is older now."

Mr. Johnson interrupted our conversation as I see him waltzing in. He was walking a little slow. But had some pep in his step.

"Hello Mr. Johnson, what are you doing out of bed?"

"You know I wouldn't miss my star person returning to work. We miss you around here."

"Awe thanks, Mr. Johnson. I missed you too."

"You know, I never liked that husband of yours. Are you still with him?"

"Yes, we are still married Mr. Johnson."

I ignored that last comment. He had been against me marrying him since the day we met. Mr. Johnson was a black man, who was wise beyond his years. The cancer had taken a toll on his physical health but he was still as wise as they came. He left the company to me when he became too sick to continue to manage it. As long as I was staying at home my husband was authorized to act as CEO of the company in my absence.

"Jamie, I wanted you to meet Shawna because I think you two can do good business together. I've been training Shawna since she was 18 years old, and Jamie has been my shadow for a long time. I believe you two can take the company places where it hasn't been yet. Shawna, I just don't think your husband can do that. There has not been any growth since he has been running the company. We have been stagnant for awhile. I still keep up with the financials of the company and you should too. It your company too Shawna. He tossed me the portfolio that represented the company's earning over the last 5 years."

I couldn't believe what I was looking at. I skimmed over most of the numbers. There was enough information to tell me that there was a lot of money going out, but not nearly as much return. I wondered what my husband was doing all of these years. I didn't want Mr. Johnson to think I was concerned, so I brushed it off.

"I'm glad that you're back, because now we can get things rolling. We can run a multi-billion-dollar company and with you two by my side, we will be able to do so."

"Multi-billion-dollar company, Mr. Johnson? If I am reading correctly I only see a few multi-millions."

"You're missing the bigger picture Shawna. I wanted to wait until you were back before we got everything rolling. I have some other investors. One's that are overseas and are going to help you and Jamie take this company to the next level. I didn't want to tell you until you were back on board. Please don't tell your husband about these investors. These are solely for our company only. I think partnering with your husband's firm was a bad for business. Since we have them, we might as well use them."

"What do you mean Mr. Johnson? I thought they could boost revenue and returns, now you're saying it was a bad business decision?"

"Shawna, let's just say I trusted the word of someone I knew and now we are about to be bankrupt." He cut his eyes at me. I didn't know if that comment was directed towards me or a thought aloud.

"Those numbers I showed you were up until last year, take a look at these numbers from last month. Once we are bankrupt, we can restart our firm from the ground up, and end our contract with S&A. Shawna, I need to be sure that you can keep this a secret, even from your husband until everything is finalized."

"I sure can Mr. Johnson."

I was weary. My head was spinning, there was only money left to stay open maybe another month. What the hell was my husband doing? What happened to the revenue and the business? Why didn't he tell me?

"Now Shawna once things are finalized with the bankruptcy. You will appear to your husband that you have lost your job too. You and Jamie will run the company 50/50 split, just you and Jamie, not your husband. The contract will be written as such. If anything is to happen to you Jamie will have sole ownership of the company, and vice versa. He will not be authorized to be acting CEO if you are unable to fulfill your duties. Your husband is not to have anything to do with this company, do we understand?"

"Yes, Mr. Johnson." Everything was such a blur I couldn't even think straight.

"Let me get this straight Mr. Johnson, you are giving me 50% over this new company. I am not to tell my husband till the bankruptcy is finalized, and this new contract is solid correct?" I had to repeat it aloud to ensure I heard everything correctly.

"Correct, my dear."

When I arrive back home, I didn't know how I was going to keep this secret. But it appears that my husband has been keeping some secrets too. How much money do we have? Are we bankrupt too? Has he been stealing money from the company? I feel like I can't trust him right now. Terrance walks in and interrupts my thoughts.

"Hey baby, how was your first day back at work?"

"It was good, just went over the things that I've missed."

"I want to take you and TJ out to dinner tonight, so you don't have to cook."

"Let me freshen up a bit." I had a headache, but I didn't want to seem stressed out. I had to put my game face on.

I must have had a few too many glasses of wine and it made me horny. Dinner was lovely, my husband just seemed to surprise me when I least expect it. We returned home and TJ was knocked out. Terrance begins kissing me on my neck. Hmmmm, I haven't felt this way in a long time. I instantly get wet, he begins massaging my breasts, I let out a low moan. I had a few drinks and I began to feel the effect.

"Ooh Terrance that feels so good."

Terrance began undressing me piece by piece, and then planting kisses all over my body. It felt like my body was on fire I just wanted to feel him inside of me.

"Fuck me, fuck me now Terrance!"

"Wait, " he whispered.

He turned me around and began licking from my neck down to my spine to the crack of my ass and stopped. He grabbed my ass cheeks and spread them open. He began licking the inside of my ass, that shit felt so good. I started screaming for more. He bent me over and began rubbing the head of his dick near my ass. He didn't put it in my ass, but tonight I would have been willing to do anything. He slides his rock hard dick inside of me. Oooh shit I almost forgot how big he was. It filled me up inside. I moaned in ecstasy, I immediately came all over his dick. He fucked me harder, then slower, then faster, and then slower. I came so hard I squirted all over the bed. He was still fucking me, after I squirted I couldn't take anymore. After I couldn't take anymore he got some lube and put it in my ass. I flinched a little but I didn't want to ruin the mood. I figured I might as well give him what he wants. After a few minutes of anal sex, he comes hard inside my ass and collapses on top of me.

As I laid under Terrance, I remembered that we haven't had sex in almost 6 months. All kinds of thoughts began to run through my mind. Was he cheating? Has he ever cheated? I never questioned it until now because he never gave me a reason to. Terrance looked so peaceful sleeping, I let him sleep, and dozed off in his arms.

Terrance

My wife came home all happy and shit about returning to work. I hadn't seen her that happy in a very long time. It was sad that it was coming to an end. I didn't know how to tell her that her company is going broke and that it will be shut down in a month. Did I have something to do with it? Partially, Brian and I had been pulling their investors from their firm for awhile now. When we convinced them that they were going broke, it was easy for them to make the decision to partner with us. I haven't even told her that my company is planning to pull out of the firm. I haven't decided when the right time to tell her was. I know she will be devastated, but things happen for a reason.

I decided that I was going to take her and TJ out for dinner to her favorite Mexican restaurant. Dinner was fantastic, and my wife appeared to be enjoying herself a bit too much. I noticed after the 5th glass of wine, she was feeling herself. She kept rubbing on my dick through my pant at the dinner table. I hadn't felt myself get this hard around my wife in a very long time. I was thinking I might get lucky tonight. I wasn't going to get my hopes up. She had a glow to her that I hadn't seen since before TJ was born.

I made love to her that night, and I gave her what she deserved from me. I quickly noticed after she squirted my dick began to soften. I didn't know what to do, because that had never happened to me before. I began fucking her in her ass, my wife doesn't like it too much but seeing her ass jiggle when I'm hitting it makes me hard again. After 3 minutes, I feel myself about to explode. That was the best sex I've ever had with my wife in a long time. I forgot how good the pussy really was. I may never cheat again as long as I can get it like this at least 3-4x's a week.

I doze off, and wake up to my phone vibrating on my side of the bed. Shawna is cuddled under me and looks so peaceful sleeping. The text reads:

"Hey sexy I've been thinking about you since I saw you at the gym... can't wait to see you again."

I wondered who it could be. Before you go judging me, I meet a lot of people at the gym. Yes, I do give my number out a lot. I responded:

"Who is this?"

Several minutes later, I get a response:

"So, you don't remember me at the gym. You stared a long time at my ass and it seemed like you were checking me out on the treadmill too."

Ah damn it's Jamie, I almost forgot. I've been waiting for Jamie to text or call, I honestly almost forgot. My dick immediately got rock hard again. Shawna begins to fidget around.

"Hey honey, everything ok?"

"Yea I'm good just still a little horny baby. You think you can take care of that for me?"

To my surprise, Shawna gets on all fours and goes up under the cover and begins what feels like she is sucking the skin of my dick. She starts jiggling my balls, and deep throating, damn that shit feels so good. I drop my phone. It seemed like I almost immediately came in her mouth. She swallowed it all. I was in awe.

"You like that baby?"

"You damn right! I love that shit!"

"Where have you been all my life?" She chuckles. I forgot all about Jamie, because I think I just got my wife back! Maybe I need get her drunk more often.

I wake up to the sound of my alarm clock blaring in my ear, and Shawna not beside me. I forgot she went back to work and I have to take TJ to school. I look at my phone, it's dead. I plug it up, wait till it has some juice to cut it on. Meanwhile, I go wake TJ up.

"Hey buddy, it's time to get up!"

"Oh daddy, I don't wanna go to school anymore those kids are still picking with me daddy!"

"You said you and mommy were going to talk to Principal Toler."

"TJ when did this happen?"

"Yesterday daddy! The teacher even put me in the timeout chair for hitting the other boy daddy. I didn't mean to, but he was being so mean to me, calling me all types of mean names. In history, we learned those names are mean and only mean people say those words."

"Well son, I will be up to school today again to talk to Principal Toler."

It brought tears to my eyes for my son to have witness any of this. Principal Toler was beginning to piss me off, after he said he was going to fix this situation, looks like he didn't. It looks like he just made it worse. I rushed out of the house to go to the school.

"Yes sir, how may I help you?"

"Principal Toler, please?"

"May I ask who you are sir?"

"Let him know Mr. James is here."

"Ok, have a seat and I will call him for you."

Principal Toler immediately comes out and greets me. I wasn't here for the pleasantries.

"Ah Mr. James, how are you today?"

His smile turned into a frown when he realized Shawna wasn't with me.

"Not so good Toler, we need to talk now."

"Mr. James follow me to my office."

"How can I help you today?"

"Well, Toler I came in last week about my son being bullied at your school. You told me you would handle it. But this morning my son tells me that he is still being bullied. In fact he got in trouble for hitting one of the boys."

"Ah yes, Mr. James he did receive a reprimand for the assault on the young boy. As I told you before there is really nothing I can do. His parents pay tuition just like you do Mr. James."

"Cut the bullshit Toler, I'm not fucking with you. I was in his face. "This is my son we are talking about. Expel the fuckers for all I care, or I will make sure someone else has your seat before the week is out." It was an idle threat, but I wanted to make sure he knew I was serious.

"Look Terrance there isn't anything I can do, these children's parents are charitable donors too. My hands are tied. I wish I could do more but I can't. His voice was softer and we were more impersonal."

I hated to do it to Toler, but I made my idle threat.

"Ok…. Toler you just made your bed, I hope you are prepared to lay in it."

"Is that a threat, Terrance?"

"Nah, Toler it's a promise."

I made the idle threat because I wanted him to know I was serious. Me and Toler go way back, I couldn't do it to him, but if I had to I would. My child came first. As soon as I left, I made a few phone calls to the Superintendent of the school.

"Yes, may I speak with Dana Thomas please?"

"Hey Dana, it's Terrance how are you doing?" Dana started going on and on about how I didn't call. I had to block that shit out.

"I know. I know. But listen I need a favor."

"What is it Terrance?"

"I'm having a few issues with Principal Toler over here at the school. I need you to pull a few strings, to get him suspended or even fired."

"Why…. Terrance? What did he do?"

"My son is a product of bullying, and before I do anything drastic. I want to take another route."

"Well, you know we are trying to crack down on bullying, put in a formal complaint with the School Board. I'll pull it, and I will call you for a meeting by the end of the week. I don't know about fired, but we can definitely raise some red flags for you."

"Thanks babe. I owe you."

"Hmm hmm, whatever Terrance."

I head to the office and it's almost 10:00 a.m. I called Brian and let him know I'm was on the way.

"Hey my man, I'm on the way. I had to take care of some things at the school."

"It's cool, just get here. We need to sit down and talk."

I wanted to tell my wife what's going on with her company. But I know she will run and tell Mr. Johnson so I'll just wait until shit hits the fan. I couldn't stand that old man and I was pretty sure he didn't like me either. Brian has been my partner since we were knee high to a duck. He has definitely been the back bone to the company, even when I didn't know everything.

"About time you got here." Brian said.

"Yea, yea I know, I apologize."

"We need to sit down and talk Terrance, shit is about to hit the fan real fast. We have to pull out fast they are losing money left and right. If they find out what we're doing, we might be in court. They can sue us for backing out the contract, but that sure as hell less to lose then if we stay with them."

"I thought you said we had a month tops?" Brian directly didn't know that we had made the setup for them to go bankrupt. I mean we had to build our partnerships and business too. Business is business.

"Yea, I know but I've been looking at the numbers again, and again. I don't know how they are affording to stay open. We need to speak with Mr. Johnson like yesterday."

"You know Mr. Johnson has money. He is probably using his own money to stay open."

"Get him on the phone and we'll talk to him, because we are losing money by the day Terrance."

This day just seems to get worse and worse. I kept thinking that I would have time to tell Shawna about what is happening. She will find out when she gets home today.

"Aight man, we scheduled to meet with Mr. Johnson at 2:00 p.m. today."

Shawna

I ran out the house this morning. I was running late. I was sitting at my desk with my head down thinking about last night. It was such a blur; I can't believe I drank so much. I think I had a hangover. Terrance and I haven't had sex like that in so long, I forgot how good it was. I need THAT sex back in our life.

"Shawna, can you meet me in the conference room?" Jamie snapped me out of my thoughts.

"Sure, be there in 5 minutes." I grabbed my notepad and favorite ink pen.

"How's everything going?"

"Not so good, Shawna your husband's firm is pulling out much sooner than we thought. We are waiting on Mr. Johnson to arrive. He says he has something in mind."

"What? Why?"

"Probably for the same reason we are filing for bankruptcy. They would rather take the penalty, than to stay in business with us any longer."

Mr. Johnson walks in, he looks a little healthier than I've seen before.

"Hey Shawna, Jamie, we don't have a lot of time before I meet with your husband and his partner. But this… this is good that they are pulling out."

"How is it good?" I asked naïve to some of the business strategies that Mr. Johnson has been in longer than I've been alive.

"Well, Shawna this is good. If they pull out before the bankruptcy is filed which I was on the way to the courthouse to do now. We can sue them! Say hello to your advance bonuses!" He said with the biggest smile I've ever seen.

I looked over to Jamie who has this wide grin. While I'm still looking dumbfounded. Jamie stepped in and explains everything.

"When you and your husband sat down to write the contract. There was a clause that stipulated in the agreement that if they did not fulfill their terms of the agreement that they would have to pay a penalty of $3.5 million. The $3.5 million is extra for the company because we already have the money to fund the new company."

"In terms of the money, you and Jamie will split everything 50/50. I will make sure that the check is cut to myself and once all of the papers are signed and filed, you both will receive your share." Mr. Johnson says.

Inside I was happy as hell. I just became $1.75 million dollars richer. But something was telling me to not to tell Terrance about the money, or what was happening. It was a gut feeling, something I never went against. It's the same feeling I had when I stepped down from work. I ignored that feeling and look where it has gotten me.

I noticed Jamie smiling from ear to ear. Out of nowhere Jamie asks. "So how long have you been married?"

"I've been married for eight years. We moved kind of fast."

"Aww, that's nice, marriage is a beautiful thing."

"Thanks, we have our ups and downs. We are still making it through."

I sat in deep thought reflecting on our marriage, it does seem like we have had more downs than ups recently. I returned to my office to check my bank accounts, something that I haven't done since TJ was born. I figured I might as well keep up with the money now since I have returned to work. But I noticed that the passwords to the accounts have been changed. I click forgot password then check my email. Well the email hasn't changed on the account. I don't check that email associated with that account often. We have joint accounts but I still have my personal account that does not show on online banking. I notice the balance on our joint account is $112,885.43. I expected us to have more. I check the withdrawals and noticed checks written and cash withdrawals. One check was written for $5,000. I click on the image and realize that it is written to a Latonya Billiard. I began to become suspicious because it was just a few weeks ago. Who the hell is Latonya Billiard? There had to be a good explanation. I continued to scroll through and realized there are many more checks written to the same person and a few cash withdrawals of $500.00. What the hell was my husband doing? I called to check my single account, and the balance was still the same plus interest as $6,004,

485.45. The account balance was still the same. But I could never be too sure. I never gave Terrance access to that account, even though I told him he had access to it. I had to figure out who the hell is Latonya Billiard.

Jamie stepped into my office interrupting my thoughts.

"You want to get some lunch?"

"Sure, it's this Japanese spot off of 42nd street." Jamie offered to pay for lunch. I was definitely jumping at the idea of going.

Jamie and I made small talk. It was awkward because I never had a partner other than Mr. Johnson. We both discussed how Mr. Johnson became a part of our lives. We both described Mr. Johnson as a fatherly figure. Jamie talked about learning everything about the business from Mr. Johnson and I discussed how Mr. Johnson became my mentor. Jamie appeared to be a down to earth person that I began to vibe with well.

Once back at the office, my mind wondered back to these different checks written to this Latonya Billiard and multiple cash withdrawals. My mind was flooded in thoughts. I tried not to become paranoid, or be insecure. I would make this a mental note to ask him about it in the near future. But right now, I have to focus on this new deal that Mr. Johnson is currently pursuing. I looked at my watch and it is well after 2:00 p.m. I have a feeling I will be working late so I texted Terrance to ask him to pick up TJ from school.

"Hey baby I hope your day is going well. I am going to be at work late today can you pick up TJ?"

He responded back immediately:

"Yeah is everything ok?"

I thought to myself, why wouldn't everything be ok? I responded:

"Yeah baby everything is good."

I continued to work on some portfolios for the new investment firm, the numbers look great. It was almost too good to be true. Jamie interrupted my thoughts.

"Hey Shawna, are you busy?"

"Nope, what's up? I was just looking over these portfolios, and thinking that the numbers look really good, almost too good to be true." I was having déjà vu. I remembered saying those words eight years ago.

"I was just thinking the same thing myself. Have you seen the numbers for the last 5 years?"

Jamie and I began to talk endlessly about random things from relationships, friendships, work, school, siblings. We both realized that Mr. Johnson hadn't come back to the office. Jamie called Mr. Johnson and he explained that he would see us in the morning. He had some other things to take care of. It was now well after 6:00 p.m. Jamie and I ordered Chinese for dinner and I wanted to finish talking about expansion of the company. We were thinking with the new company we will need at least 150 more employees. But we will keep the current employees, although several employees have turned in their resignation notice already. First thing on the agenda tomorrow was an all employee meeting. After the busy day I had today, it was definitely hard to be focused, from the company, to my husband it was all seeming like it was going south. I get up to leave and didn't even hear Jamie come up behind me. Jamie comes up behind me and begins to kiss my neck, and whispers in my ear.

"I can do things to your that your husband has never done, I can take you places that he can't." As Jamie continued to lick around my neck and bite my ear.

"Wait... I can't do this.... I've never done this before."

"It's ok, I'll be gentle. I just think you are so attractive, and I couldn't take my eyes off of you all day."

Before I could say no, Jamie was already fingering me, while kissing me all over my neck and breasts. Jamie pushes me on the desk and raises my skirt and begins to pull my thong off and licking my pussy like it was a pussy eating marathon. I realized what was happening.

"I can't.... I'm sorry.... I can't.... I've never done this before. We are partners.... my husband.... I can't. I'm sorry."

"No, Shawna, I'm sorry. I never should have crossed that line with you. I'm sorry." Jamie walked out.

I spent my whole drive home thinking about Jamie, I've never had my pussy eaten like that before, not even by my

husband. It was definitely…..different. Jamie was so
gentle, soft and careful with my body, nothing like my
husband. It was a different experience. I have had some
experiences in college but nothing like the one I had today.

I get home and realized that I don't have any panties on.
How was I going to get pass Terrance with this one? I'll tell
him it has been a long day and I need to take a shower, so I
could just keep walking. I noticed him sitting on the couch.

"Hey baby, it's been a long day. I just want a nice hot
bath." I leaned over to kiss him and he grabbed my ass.

"I cooked dinner, it's your favorite."

"Baby I'm sorry, I had dinner at the office tonight. I'll take
it for lunch tomorrow."

I waltzed pass Terrance and made it to the bathtub without
him noticing. I hope he didn't notice. I drifted off to sleep
in the Jacuzzi tub and was awakened by Terrance. "C'mon
babe, you fell asleep, you must have had a long day."

Terrance carried me to the bed, dries me off, and puts the
covers over me.

Terrance

I got a text from Shawna asking me to pick up TJ. This shit was getting old real quick. I can't wait until we get out of this deal with them so Shawna can stay at home. The deal with Mr. Johnson went well. It turned out that we have to pay a $3.5-million-dollar penalty for pulling out the contract. Brian said that we would lose more if we stayed in the contract. We may have taken a loss upfront, but we definitely can get the money back. I don't know how to break the news to Shawna. I wondered has Mr. Johnson told her yet? Would she tell me if he did? Tonya was blowing my phone up lately. Had it been that long since I paid her? Maybe I needed to talk to her. I tried to log onto the online banking. I realized the password has been changed. I tried again and again. Then I locked myself out. My thoughts started racing. I immediately began to think that Shawna has seen the bank account. I know some shit is about to go down tonight as many checks I have written to Tonya. I knew I should have paid her cash. I didn't anticipate on Shawna going back to work so soon. Damn it! I get a text from Jamie, I realized that a week had passed since the last message from Jamie, and it said:

"Hey baby wyd? I'm hot, horny and waiting for you."

If this shit goes sour with Shawna tonight, I might be over there after all. I responded back:

"I'm chillin…oh word? What do you want me to do about that?"

Immediately after I sent that text, Shawna walked through the door looking physically and mentally tired. She gives me a kiss, and I grab her ass and realize she doesn't have on any panties. I second guess it and think that she could be wearing a thong. Damn, Terrance stop being paranoid just because you cheating doesn't mean she is. She did look tired. When I went upstairs, she fell asleep in the tub. I carried her to the bed. I was horny, and I didn't want to wake Shawna. I'll send her a text to let her know I went to the gym after I put TJ to bed. I sent Jamie a text:

"What's your address? I'm coming through to tear that ass up."

Jamie responds almost immediately.

"43445 Island Terrace."

I get ready and put on gym gear. I send Shawna a text:

"Hey babe went to the gym be back later."

I jumped in my truck, and head over to Jamie's. It said it's a 35-minute drive. I pulled up to Jamie's place, Jamie lived in a nice subdivision in a nice ass house similar mine. Jamie answered the door in a silk robe.

"Hey baby, took you long enough. I've been waiting for you to show me what you're working with."

"Is that right?"

My dick was rock hard and I could hardly wait. Jamie was showing off those legs just like before and had a nice juicy ass to go with it. Jamie led me to the bedroom, and had one of those California King size beds. Jamie's house was definitely decked out. I laid across the bed.

"What's up, you gon' come get this dick or not?"

"You know I am baby." As Jamie seductively began to strip for me. I wasn't into all of that. I just wanted some ass.

Jamie crawled on the bed and begins kissing me from my neck down to the head of my dick, and begins to circle the head of my dick and then takes it all in. That shit felt so good, I've never had head like this. I was ready to cum and I hadn't even hit it yet. Jamie tells me to turn over.

"Huh?" I looked confused and nervous.

"Nah I'm not turning over." Jamie tells me again to turn over.

"Nobody is going to hurt you."

"Now I ain't for that gay shit, nobody sticking nothing in my ass, fingers, tongues or nothing." I must admit I was a little nervous. I didn't know what Jamie was going to do. But tonight, I was feeling experimental. Jamie began licking down the middle of my back right at the crack of my ass and stopped. Then grabs my ass checks spread them wide apart and begins licking around my asshole and sticking the tongue in. I jumped and I tried to squeeze my ass cheeks back together.

"Relax," Jamie said.

That shit felt so good, I've never had anyone not even my wife do anything like that. I couldn't take it anymore. I tell

Jamie to bend over and let me hit it from behind. I had to admit Jamie's ass looked so fat. I thought I was about to cum from just looking at that ass. I put my dick in and it was so tight. I feel myself about to bust immediately. I had to pace myself, come on Terrance. Shit, fuck it. I explode all over the bed.

"Damn baby, that's all you got?" Jamie said. I ignored that comment. I grabbed my pants as I sit on the edge of the bed, shaking my head at myself. Damn, did I just cum that quick?

"I'll see you later aight."

Jamie looked disappointed.

"What am I just a booty call? It's cool, the dick wasn't that good anyway."

"You knew what it was when you gave me your number. I wasn't really looking for a booty call, more of a friends with benefits kinda thing."

"Actually, no I didn't know what you were looking for because you never told me. It's nice to know that's where we stand."

I admit it hurt my ego a little. I wasn't going to let Jamie know that. I ain't got time for all that sensitive shit. I looked over Jamie who is already dressed watching the game, which got my attention.

"I didn't know you watched basketball."

"Yea the Heat is my team, you ain't know? I'ma watch them smash the Pacers."

The shit talking began. I admit that Jamie was more than I expected. We sat watched the game, ate popcorn. I noticed Jamie wanted to cuddle under me. It wasn't bad at all. It felt too much like cheating to me. I didn't do the emotional part. It's just about the nut Terrance, don't get caught up.

"Aight look Jamie, I gotta bounce. I'ma holla at you later." I left reflecting on that moment.

"When will I see you again?"

"Soon."

I got back home, Shawna was still asleep, which meant she didn't get my text message. That was good because I didn't want her questioning why I came home so late. But I wondered why she didn't question me about the account? Someone could have hacked our accounts. I'm going to have to go to the bank first thing tomorrow morning to be sure. That would be unlike Shawna not to say anything about that. She definitely would have been all up in my shit. I looked over at how beautiful Shawna is and wondered where did we go wrong? How did I get here, the lying, the cheating, the sneaking behind her back? She was good to me, but I'm still doing her wrong. We have had our ups and downs, but overall she has been a good wife to me. I gotta be a better man Terrance, this shit is getting old. A text interrupted my thoughts.

"You betta give me a call right now or I'ma tell ur wife all about our little affair."

There was only other person that would text me this late. It was Tonya. I'ma hit her off with some money, this time doing it cash and leave that shit alone. She was becoming a pain in my ass. I had been fucking with her too long. I gotta admit though, Tonya was loyal. She could have blew my shit along time ago, but she didn't. I should probably give her more this time. Jamie became the center of my thoughts. I thought about leaving her before when shit got real rough. But I'm still here. Terrance, snap out of it man, you lusting over this Jamie and you only hit it one time. That one time was enough to leave me reminiscing.

Jamie

Shawna was so attractive. I know I crossed all types of lines tonight. I had to see what she tasted like, and just as expected it was good. I wanted to go further, but she just kept saying her husband. Fuck him! If he didn't know how to please her, I did. I can take her places that he never will. I hope it won't be weird at work tomorrow. We gotta get down to business. After that little escapade with Shawna, I was all hot and horny. I texted my little play toy that I met a few weeks ago. I was waiting to text Terrance, because I didn't want him to think I was thirsty. But to my surprise he was feeling the same way I was. I wanted to do some freaky things to Terrance, and take him places he had never been before.

Terrance came over. I admired his chocolate self, he definitely had the body of a God. I couldn't help myself. I was definitely going to turn him out tonight. I had Terrance screaming like a little girl in that submissive position. I knew he like that shit, he just didn't want to admit it but it's cool. I always get my man. It was just a matter of time. When it was time to perform, he was so eager to get in it that he came fast. I know how to fix that next time, he wasn't ready for all that.

I turned on the Heat game. That seemed to get his attention. We shit talked, and ate popcorn the whole game after realizing he was a big basketball fan. It didn't seem like he liked cuddling all that much, I guess it was too much of an emotional attachment. But I wasn't looking for a man right now anyway. He was going to be a good friend with benefits, at least that what he said. Most men fall for me anyway. I have that effect on people. But that Terrance, I definitely have to get another piece of him. I laying in my bed wondering if he was married or had kids. We never had that conversation. I don't think we ever will.

I already know what you think of me. How can someone as fine as me want to go both ways? Easy, I'm selfish, sometimes the same sex isn't enough. Sometimes I want dick, sometimes I want pussy. But tonight, I was being greedy. Shawna got me all hot and bothered, I needed Terrance to finish it. I hope Shawna lets me taste that sweet pussy of hers again.

Shawna

I glanced over at the clock, it says 1:52 a.m., I feel for Terrance and he wasn't there. I reached for my phone and realized that I received a text from him at 9:14 p.m. saying he was going to the gym. I know the gym he goes to is a 24 hour. He normally doesn't stay out that long. I immediately call him. But his phone goes straight to voicemail. I walked into TJ's room to make sure everything is ok. I return back to our bedroom, and lay back down. It was an exhausting day, all I could think about was how good Jamie ate my pussy. It was making me all wet again. I shouldn't be having these thoughts, I'm married. I heard Terrance come into the bedroom, I pretended I was asleep. He goes and takes a shower nothing different from what he normally does except it's later than he usually comes in. I heard the water stop running and I turned on my side to make sure he doesn't see that I was awake. I heard his phone vibrate, and wondered who could be texting him this time of night. I'm starting to think I'm getting paranoid. First the money missing out of our account, now he was getting home late from the gym and now the text messages and phone calls. Could Terrance be cheating on me? I shifted my thoughts. There was one point in my marriage that I thought he was. It didn't last long. I shifted a little in the bed just enough to make him think I might be waking up. He immediately rolls over and puts his arms around me.

I woke up much earlier before Terrance the next morning. Truth is, I couldn't sleep because of my paranoia. I got TJ up for school and made breakfast for him. I was in a relatively good mood despite my paranoid thoughts. My first stop was the bank. I needed to know who this Latonya chick was. Terrance interrupted my thoughts.

"Hey babe, you're up early?"

"Yeah, I have to be at the office early this morning to go over some things with Mr. Johnson."

"Is everything ok?"

"Everything is fine."

"Why would something be wrong?"

"Nothing, I just wanted to be sure."

"Hey hun, can you take TJ to school? I need to get to this meeting on time."

"Sure babe. See you later, love you."

"Love you, too."

I arrived to the bank just as they opened. I needed to do some investigating. I had to play everything cool with Terrance. I had to let him know that he didn't have the upper hand. This older lady greeted me.

"Hello, would I be able to speak to a financial representative in regards to my account?"

"Sure, how can we help you today?"

"Well, I'm not sure. Yesterday I was reviewing our joint account for the first time in years, and noticed there were personal checks written to a Latonya Billiard. I would like to know who wrote these checks, because I do not know this person at all."

"Ok, Mrs. James, let's look at your account. I need some personal information. What is you date of birth, address and account number?"

I disclose the information to the representative. I'm just hoping that this is all a misunderstanding and my husband hasn't been writing checks to some bitch.

"Ok, I do see where there have been multiple checks written out to Ms. Billard. Let's see if we can find out who wrote them through our imaging program. It definitely could be a possible that fraudulent activity has occurred on this account. Mrs. James, it looks like your husband personally wrote out these checks, and I have found that they date back almost five years. It appears to be a monthly transaction taking place between the 25th-30th of each month."

I was definitely lost in my thoughts. I became tearful.

"Is there anything else unusual on my account? Could you print those checks out for me?"

"The only other thing I see that is unusual is the amount of money being transferred to an outside account on the 10th of each month in the amount of $10,500.00. Let's see if I can take a look at when this began happening. This appears to be dated back for about five years also."

"Can you tell me the name on this outside account?"

As the representative continued to talk I was becoming more pissed off as the conversation continued. Terrance is not only stealing from me. He is also writing checks to a bitch every month?

Does he have a second family or something? Is he living a double life? I know I haven't been working, but I still received a substantial monthly income to cover most of the bills. In addition to monthly rent from my tenants. The representative interrupted my thoughts.

"I am unable to tell you the name of the outside account. We do not have access to this information."

Where was his money that is supposed to be deposited into our account?

"Ma'am could you see if there have been any other direct deposits into this account, other than my own?"

"No ma'am there hasn't. Actually I only see one transaction for an absorbent amount three years ago for $100,000."

As I was running all of this through my mind, so that means he has been stealing from me, a few years after TJ was born. The 100k that is in the account was from money that my grandmother left me when she passed. I haven't been working since TJ was born, my income was still at $12,000 a month despite not physically working. It would be much higher if I was. Then he has the nerve to give me an allowance? That would mean we only have $12,000 in the account? I just received my paycheck last week from the company. As I was running all of the numbers through my head, something I always prided myself in.

"Ma'am is there anything else I can help you with today?"

"Yes, actually you can. I need whatever is remaining in that account to be transferred into my personal account. In addition, I need my direct deposit to stop going into this account. I will make the change at my place of employment. We have another two weeks before I receive another paycheck, which will be more than enough time to change this information."

"Sure, ma'am that is done. Is there anything else I can help you with today?"

"No ma'am, I think I am done today."

I left the bank feeling satisfied, I couldn't even fathom thinking that my husband for all these years has been stealing from me. This is the game he wants to play. I return back home, remembering I forgot to grab my heels. I knew Terrance had left already with TJ. It was still early, and he probably went to work.

As I arrived back at the house. I realized there was a notice on my door stating that if $12,690.42 is not paid by the end of the day today our house will be foreclosed upon. My mind was spinning, what the fuck? Our mortgage was only $2200.00 a month. This fucker hasn't even been paying the bills? I swear I was about to lose it. My mind started racing a million miles a minute. I was fuming, the ghetto was about to come out of me, but I wasn't going to let Terrance know. I have millions coming in and his ass is about to have nothing. I snatched the notice off the door and wondered what in the hell else could go wrong today. I needed to call Mr. Johnson, and let him know I will be late to the meeting. After I get off the phone, I run back to my car, and haul ass to the bank. Our mortgage was with a different bank, I began asking them how long has my mortgage been unpaid. The lady rants off some information, and continues to speak to me in this condescending tone.

"Well, Mrs. James your mortgage has not been paid in over six months and if the balance is not paid today. We will move forward with the foreclosure."

"Will you accept a check?"

"No ma'am only a cashier's check, no personal checks."

I was becoming frustrated, but luckily my bank is right across the street. I looked over, and it looks like Terrance's car parked right in front of the bank. He looked like he was pissed. I waited a moment, because now I know he has put two and two together and probably was going to call me. I watched him and waited until he sped off. I literally run across the street to let the teller know that I need a cashier's check for $13,000 to come out of my personal checking account. She asked for my ID, and keys some numbers, then asks is there anything else she could help me with. I answered no, quickly.

I returned to pay my mortgage. The same lady asked if she could help me, I responded that I was there to pay the amount on my mortgage. The same lady that spoke to me in such a condescending tone looked surprised when I returned with a cashier's check for $13,000.

"Could you tell me whose name is on the mortgage? It should be me and my husband. But I noticed that only my name was on the foreclosure notice?" I noticed the lady's tone had change since I returned with the money.

"Sure, Mrs. James you are the only one listed on the mortgage. It appears that Mr. James removed himself about 6 months ago." This fucker! What the fuck was going on six months ago that he felt the need to remove himself from the mortgage? Was he about to leave me or something?

"Thank You, everything is ok with my house now, correct?"

"Yes ma'am it is. We will stop the foreclosure proceedings."

This was definitely the day from hell. I waltzed into the office looking like I already has a busy day. I complete these things before 10:00 a.m. I didn't even get to my office before Lisa was saying that Jamie and Mr. Johnson were in Conference Room 1.

"Shawna, I'm glad you could make it." Mr. Johnson says.

"Mr. Johnson, you have no idea the shit I'm going through right now. Excuse my language. I'll inform you later. I sure hope you can guide me through this."

Mr. Johnson was the like the father I never had.

"Will do Shawna. We will talk later." He winked.

"Alright, down to business. They have pulled out of the contract and paid the penalty of the $3.5 million. I have cashed it and here are both your cashier's check. We will continue to proceed with the bankruptcy. The papers have been filed, and we will be holding a staff meeting today to inform them of the changes. We will inform them and offer them options. If they stay on board with us, they will be receiving an employee bonus for being a loyal employee. If they choose not to, we will pay them severance. I've heard a lot of rumors in the office so now it is time to lay them to rest. I know some of our loyal employees will stay with us. But some see the ship sinking and will jump ship. It is time to weed out those that aren't loyal to us. When we move forward, it's just you two now." I looked over at Jamie and became a little nervous with the future plans.

We held the staff meeting in the conference room. I looked around. I saw new staff, old staff and wondered who would leave. As it turned out, about 40 of our staff left. They were relatively new employees. They would not receive much of a severance, but something was better than nothing. The 40 that resigned expressed that they were going with the company we formerly partnered with. I glanced around the table and saw uncertainty in our employee's eyes. I tried to reassure them without giving them too much information.

"We will keep our doors open as long as we can. We want to ensure that you will continue to receive a paycheck until we make this transition. I am sending a copy of a confidentiality notice around. We do not need to remind you of how important it is to keep any information that we disclose confidential. There is a fine, and possible incarceration for breach of confidentiality. This transition should be complete within the next month or so. Thank you for your cooperation."

I could feel Jamie staring at me as I was talking. It made me a bit nervous. I watched everyone look at the confidentiality notice. Some looked confused while others just signed it and left the meeting.

"I do not need to remind you the importance of this confidentiality agreement. If you do not sign this agreement I will take that as your resignation." I added.

I see a few more employees signing the agreements and then the remaining.

"Thank you, you are free to leave for the day." I gathered the remaining confidentiality agreements from the table. Jamie began giving feedback about the meeting.

"Nice job Shawna. It was good to be able to weed out those that were not going to be loyal to us. Those were the weaker links anyway, they wouldn't have been beneficial to us. We will rehire once we make this transition."

"I'm sorry, Jamie. I really need to speak with Mr. Johnson in private."

"Ok, sure we'll talk later."

"Hey Mr. Johnson can we talk?" I peeped into his office.

"Sure Shawna, you know we can always talk."

In private Mr. Johnson liked to be called Tim, especially when we weren't talking business. He was there for me when my father passed away. He was there when I married Terrance, although he was totally against it. He even walked me down the aisle. I broke down and began to cry.

"I don't know where I went wrong. My husband is cheating, lying and stealing from me." I was sobbing.

"Shawna, I don't need to tell you I told you so. I knew he was no good. You were head over hills for him. I knew nothing I could say or do would bring you out of that. But c'mon on Shawna. Cut that out, that is not the Shawna I know. Tell me what's going on."

After I catch him up with the short version of my revelation. He looks like he is in deep thought.

"Shawna, I told you I never did like him. He was never right for you."

"I know. I know." I hung my head in shame.

"You need to outsmart him. You did the right thing by taking all of your money out of the joint account. One thing he didn't count on was you finding out because you had been in the dark for so long. Now it's time to take your company, and your life back. They are thinking they did the right thing over there because they heard through the grapevine we were filing bankruptcy. I honestly wouldn't be surprised if your husband had a hand in it. Your husband is hoping that you will lose your job, depend on him and be in control again. He has controlled you, the finances and everything else all these years. Don't let him do that. You are ahead of the game. He doesn't know that you are about to own this company, and make billions. Own it Shawna!

"Ouch!" He nudged me kind of hard.

It's good that he took his name off the mortgage because now he cannot add it back without your authorization. He has no access to your personal accounts. If he is indeed broke, he will be at your beck and call. Play smart Shawna, don't let this break you. When you get home today, you know there will be an argument, argue a lot make him think you're upset, make him think you're losing your job and you're stressed. Men we like to feel like we are the providers. Once he feels like he is in control then you can drop that bombshell. Trust me Shawna, as long as your husband is a partner over there in that firm it their doors won't be open long."

I sat there in tears, reflecting on everything Tim had said. I was hurting, but I wanted to make him hurt more. He made sense a lot of sense. I can't let my emotions get the best of me. I have to control this situation. It was always something about when Mr. Johnson disappeared and Tim appeared. He always knew what to say to make everything better and I felt better too. I sat in my office looking at all the missed calls on my phone. Terrance has called 12 times already and left multiple messages with Lisa. He probably thinks I left him. I wanted him to be paranoid.

Jamie waltzes into my office and shuts the door.

"Hey Jamie, what's up?"

Jamie walked around my desk, opened my legs, pushed my skirt up and began eating my pussy. I didn't tell Jamie to stop this time, but instead pushed further. Damn, it felt so good, Jamie turned me around then began licking me from my ass to my pussy, I came all over my desk. I hope no one heard me. Jamie got up, and walked out of my office like nothing happened. I have never had my pussy eaten like that. I definitely have to make sure that happens again and again. That was random, real random. What do I have to lose now. He started this game and I was going to finish it.

Terrance

I woke up to find Shawna already out of bed. I knew she must have been exhausted. Usually I am up before she is. I wake up to several other text messages from Tonya, mostly threats. I made a mental note to take care of that situation today, after I swing by the bank. Shawna looked like she was in a hurry and asked me can I take TJ to school. She said she had a meeting with Mr. Johnson early this morning. I think today is the day she may find out she is no longer going to be working for the company. She kisses me as she hurries out the door.

"Love you hun."

As soon as she leaves, I called Dana early this morning.

"You take care of that thing, I asked you to take care of?"

"Well, Good Morning to you too Terrance. What do I get if I did?"

"Let's just say I will make it worth your while." I flirted a little.

"It's handled Terrance. When will I see you again?"

"Soon, Dana, soon." I hung up.

Principal Toler knows better not to fuck with me. I know people that know people.

I called Tonya up after I dropped TJ off at school. She answers after the 2nd ring.

"Yo, what's up with you blowing up my phone?"

"Good Morning Terrance." Tonya says in this sarcastic tone.

"Is this the only way I can get in contact with you is by threatening to tell your wife?"

"Eh look, what do you want? I can be over in a few to give you your money."

"I don't want any money Terrance. I want that dick of yours, so you need to come and give me some."

"Nah, I'm aight. As a matter of fact this isn't going to work between you and me anymore."

"Why Terrance? Did I do something? I apologize for threatening you. I didn't mean it, it was just that you weren't returning none of my phone calls, and I…"

"What Tonya! Look you are making things more difficult than they need to be! You knew my situation before you signed up for it. I have a lot going on. I can't do this anymore." And to believe 6 months ago, I was ready to leave my wife for this crazy chick.

"Ok Terrance, can we at least still be friends?" She sounded like she lost her best friend.

"Yeah, sure, whatever. I'll talk to you later."

After getting those things out of the way today. Today seemed like it would be a good day today. Tonya wasn't tripping, Dana wasn't tripping. Tonya didn't want any money. That was money I can keep in my pocket. Now I'm going to head to the bank and see what is up with our account. I don't think Shawna knows what is going on with our bank accounts. If she did, she would have ripped me a new asshole. Don't let Shawna fool you she might be all business professional, but she can bring the hood out and that was only for the right situations. I pulled up to the bank and was greeted by an older lady.

"Hello, sir how can I help you today?"

"Yes, I need to see what is going on with my account, my password was changed. I didn't do it and my wife doesn't have access. I need to make sure everything is ok with our account?"

"Ok, sure sir, your full name, date of birth and address?"

I disclosed all that information and think Shawna couldn't possibly know, could she? I've done some foul shit that I forgot about. I'm just being paranoid as I focused my attention back on the representative.

"Ah yes, the account with you and your wife correct?"

I nodded my head in agreement.

"It appears that Mrs. James was in here this morning. She requested some information on the account. It doesn't specifically notate which information she requested. She has done a transfer for the entire account balance into her personal account."

"Excuse me! What do you mean she has transferred the entire amount? Can she do that? Why did y'all allow her to do that?"

I was getting pissed. It wasn't that much money in that account. Hell, it wasn't even my money. But I was still pissed that she transferred all the money.

"Mr. James both of you are account holders and you both can do what you want with the account, withdraw, write checks, transfer money. We do not have any control over the amount of money, and who can transfer what money into their account."

"Can you transfer it back from her account? I should have access to the other account as well."

"No sir, you do not have access to this account. This is Mrs. James personal account and she has not granted you access to this account. I apologize."

"Lady, my name is on that account! I demand you transfer the money back immediately."

"No sir, you are not. I'm afraid if you do not calm down, I will have security escort you out the bank. If there is not anything else I can help you with. You have a good day."

I mean how can I get mad, it was *her* money that she transferred to her own account with the exception of a couple thousand. I stormed out of the bank with my mind going a million miles an hour. I was livid that she did it so sneakily, like right under my nose. She straight lied to my face this morning. I called Shawna to see what the fuck is going on and I get her voicemail. Shawna must know, she must know everything. I didn't plan for everything to go down this way. I thought she added me to all of her accounts. I'm pissed because that mean she is hiding something from me. Yea I'm hiding money from her too. I'm sure I have more money than her. I left the $100,000 in her account because it was hers. What kind of man would I be if I took that? Every month I was writing Tonya checks and taking $10,000 out of the account each month. Yeah, I was taking her money and paying Tonya. I know it sounds fucked up. If Shawna knows all of this, then shit is about to hit the fan. My bank account is set. I have well over 2 million in my account. But I haven't paid any of the bills, took my name of the mortgage so it would only be her responsibility. I was ready to leave her like six months ago, so I stopped paying the mortgage and I took my name off the deed. I did it so in case we did divorce it wouldn't be my responsibility. She could have the house and cars. I just didn't want to pay for it. I'll be a man and admit Tonya had me a little sprung. I even used a little bit of my money to pay her bills too. When she started showing some signs of being a little clingy and a little crazy, I began distancing myself from her.

My mind began to wonder. How much money did Shawna really have? I know she gets the profit from her townhome and I was getting her paycheck every month. That profit must be going into her personal account, because I would have known about that too. She can't have more money than me. She just can't. I was running all the numbers in my head. You can call me what you want. Shawna has been what you call, an independent woman. She has always had her own, and now I am about to take it from her and make her depend on me as a man. It made me feel inferior when we started dating and got married that she had more money than me. I got her pregnant on purpose, so she could stay home and depend on me. That backfired because Mr. Johnson was still paying her.

I'm not going to lie, I'm nervous. How much does Shawna know? I can sit here and front like I don't care. But at the end of the day as a husband I did fuck her over. Don't read this and judge me, I was trying to protect me. Shawna ain't dumb by no means. But that was when I planned to leave her. I didn't want her taking half of money, so I beat her to it. I called her again, back to back and I didn't get an answer. Was she ready to leave me? Is she at the house now? I looped back around to see if she was home. She wasn't home. I ran into the house and was relieved to see all of her things are still there. I was calculating the math in my head, Shawna couldn't have a lot of money. Yeah, I was counting her money too. She may be savvy on the business end. I think she might have about $30,000 off of the townhome and the $100,000, with the lifestyle she lives, it won't last long.

I was walking into the office, and I called her again still no answer. I was beginning to get worried because now she might leave me and take half. I forgot she has been at home for the last few years with TJ. She could seek spousal support due to her not working. I may be a selfish bastard, but there is no way I could ever go back to the lifestyle I lived before. I would pay her half.

"Hey what's up man, look like you lost your best friend or something?" Brian said.

"Nah, I'm good man just thinking about some shit."

"We gotta talk about the money we put out to get out the contract. The deal is done, we're out.... But man, I heard through the grapevine that they got over on us."

"What do you mean?" He had my attention.

"I heard that old Mr. Johnson up to something, something real big over there."

"They supposed to be bankrupt, they ain't got no money man. That little bit of chump changed we paid out ain't enough to refuel their business." I wasn't worried.

"Nah man, I heard that Mr. Johnson filing for bankruptcy was just a front. I heard they just hired somebody new to take over along with Shawna. They planning something big, heard they partnering up with some big timers overseas."

"Bullshit."

"Nah man real shit. If anything, we just probably gave Mr. Johnson over there an advancement for his new owners to take over. I'm still trying to get some more information. That is what I would do if I were him. There isn't anything we can do because we out of partnership with them. Luckily you still married to Shawna though. You get to reap those benefits man."

"Yeah for now. Man, me and Shawna might not be doing too well."

"I told you to stop fucking around on her that shit was going to catch up to you."

"Yea I know. I know. It's all good though, I'ma fix it."

Brian was my partner, my best friend, he knew everything, almost everything. He knew when I was scheming money, paying Tonya and cheating on Shawna. He knew I was about to leave Shawna for Tonya. He was the one that convinced me not to.

"Karma a bitch, don't let it fuck you over."

The deeper I got in my thoughts, I started putting everything together. Here all along I'm thinking she about to be out of work, but she about to be the owner of a bigger corporation than what she is working for. Now she just found out about what I was doing. Yeah shit just got real.

Shawna

I looked down at my phone. Terrance has called again. I was shaking my head in disgust. All this time I thought he was my husband, only to find out he has been scheming money from me, paying some hoe and using *my* money to do it. He ran my company into the ground. But shit about to change. I needed to come up with a game plan before I headed home. He doesn't know how much I know.

My mind kept going back to Jamie. I can't believe I let that happen in my office. Jamie must have thought I was some type of freak or something. My husband ain't never had a tongue game like that.

My phone begins ringing again. It was Terrance. I was livid inside, but I had to calm myself down.

"Hello."

"Hey baby, how's your day at work?"

"It's good. What's going on? What about you?"

"Nothing much, just seeing if you wanted to get a late lunch. Do you want me to bring dinner home or something?"

"Nah I'm ok, I just ate lunch." What was he digging for?

"I'm going to be home early tonight. I'll pick up TJ and I will pick up your favorite for dinner tonight."

"Ok thanks, I love you."

That was a weird conversation. He has never offered to take me to lunch even when I was working here. He probably realized that I took the money out of the account. Good.

I waltzed in the door after 6:00 p.m. I saw TJ and Terrance in front of the television watching cartoons.

"Hey, we need to talk." I saw the expression on his face turn from happy to concerned.

"What's up babe?"

"We need to go upstairs away from TJ to have this conversation." I was about to turn on the water works. I didn't want Terrance to know what I knew.

"I don't know where to start." The tears begin streaming. "I'm being laid off Terrance, and then I go to the bank today and we don't have any money. Where is all our money Terrance?"

"Babe it'll be ok you know that I am working. Why didn't you tell me you were being laid off? You know my income is sufficient to pay the bills. We will be ok. We have money Shawna a lot of it. I'll be honest I stopped putting my income in the joint account when I thought we were going to separate. Now that we are ok I'll have my income direct deposited again."

"Why didn't you tell me? Why did I have to find out like this Terrance? Moving forward, I want to be a part of the finances."

"Fine. Done. I have no problem with that."

Damn that was easier than I thought, or was he playing along with my little game. I can't believe he fell for the tears. It was easy to make him fall for the water works because I'm not a cry baby. Plan in motion, I didn't want him to know what I knew, especially about Latonya. If he finds out that I know about Latonya. He definitely will try to lie his way out of it. I am not going to worry about that right now. Right now, this has become personal.

I hope that he understands that this is war with me and him. I can't believe that he has been this deceiving me all these years.

Terrance

She finally answered the phone. I bullshit her a little bit about taking her to lunch just to pick up a vibe from her. She sounded ok. Shawna has always been the type to let her attitude and anger get the best of her. The fact that she is relatively calm says a lot. Maybe she didn't know a lot I tried convinced myself.

Shawna came in the house after six. She said she needed to talk. I was nervous. Shawna immediately broke down crying. Shawna has never been a crier, even at her grandmother's funeral, the birth of our child or even our wedding she never shed a tear. The fact that she was crying spoke volumes. It made me soften up a little bit, because she was crying. When she revealed to me she was getting laid off. I questioned Brian sources. I had to bullshit her about the money because she must not know about the checks I wrote to Tonya. I forgot to ask her about why she transferred the money out. I was so caught up with the tears that I forgot to ask. I hated to see my baby like that. I was getting a vibe not to trust her. I was trying to shake that feeling because it was my wife. She wouldn't hurt me. She wouldn't go out of her way to be deceitful. Would she? I have done all this foul shit to Shawna now I can't even think straight. I know Shawna, if Shawna knew about the checks she would have straight flipped out. She wouldn't be calm. If she knew about the money I was stealing she would definitely kill me. There was no way that she could know. Could she? My head was spinning. I went downstairs to the kitchen and pour some Brandy. I needed it after the long day I've had. I picked up my phone to call Brian. I definitely needed someone to talk to.

"Yo, my man what's up?"

'What's going on Brian?"

"Ain't shit, what's up? I paused.

"Aww shit! What happened? Did Shawna kick you out? You need a place to stay?"

"Nah just the opposite man. Shawna got laid off today. I think you are wrong about what's going on. She kind of found out about the money. I promised her that I would make her a part of the finances from now on, because you know I been scheming man. I kind of feel bad about it. Man, she cried! You know Shawna, she isn't a crier."

"Yo man don't fall for that shit! It is concrete proof that women are smarter than men. Women are emotional manipulators! Those could have been fake tears and you played right into it!"

"Nah man these weren't fake. Shawna does not cry. She didn't cry at the funeral, at our wedding or when TJ was born. She ain't no crier, so I know I must have hurt her deep."

"I hope you're right. Don't get caught up. She may know more than you think. Don't let her get over on you. Women are the masters at this game especially when they get hurt. She might not know about Tonya. But what if she does and she is waiting for you next move. Matter of fact didn't you tell me that Shawna was about to lose the house. What happened with that?"

"Oh shit! I need to down to the bank first thing tomorrow! If Shawna finds that shit out, my marriage will definitely be over. I know I ain't paid the mortgage in about six months."

"Man….. T, all I'm saying is be careful and watch her because she is watching your every move."

"I know Shawna she green to all of this. I will always be one step ahead of her."

"Aight my dude, peace."

I let all the words sink in from that converation. I started questioning everything because Shawna's actions were fucking me up. But her words were right along with her actions, anger, hurt, resentment. How much could she really know? I know first thing in the morning I need to go down to the bank.

I looked down at my phone. I got a text from Jamie. My dick immediately got hard. I ignored the first text. Then ten minutes later I get another text.

"Hey daddy you need to come over and let me suck that nice juicy dick of yours."

Damn, how could I resist that? I could feel my dick throbbing through my pants. I'm supposed to be turning over a new leaf with my wife. I wanted try with my wife first, and see if I can get some play. I wanted to make Jamie a last resort. If she wasn't in the mood, I'll have one for the road with Jamie. That would be my last time, I convinced myself. I go upstairs with my hard dick showing through my pants.

"Hey babe, look whose waiting for you." I said teasingly.

Shawna immediately sat up and had a look of disdain, but then quickly turned to seduce me. Even though she was mad at me, she giving me some ass tonight. My dick got soft as she was sucking on it. What the fuck? This couldn't be happening. But Shawna kept sucking. I was hoping she didn't notice.

"Hold up, turn over."

I know Shawna don't like me fucking her from behind. I needed to see her ass in order to get hard. As I was hitting it from behind all I did was fascinate about Jamie, so I could stay hard. This was crazy. Why couldn't my dick stay hard with my own wife? Something has to give, I felt myself about to cum. I yelled out that I was about to nut. The next thing I know she turns around and began sucking all the nut out of my dick. I'm glad I was coming because my dick was beginning to go limp again. I forgot all about Jamie. I can't let that go for too long before I lose out on some good ass.

****

The next morning, I asked Shawna to take TJ to school. She agreed. I had to go to the bank so the house wouldn't be foreclosed upon. I arrived at the bank and am greeted by a younger lady.

"Hello, how may we help you?"

"I am here to pay the mortgage. I understand we are a few months behind."

"Ok, give me a moment to pull up that account, is your name on the mortgage sir?"

"Yes it is."

"What is your name and address of the property?"

"Terrance James, 4321 Island Oak Dr., Bel Air, Maryland."

"Are you sure that your name is on the mortgage Mr. James?"

"Yes, I am positive. My wife and I purchased this home a few years ago."

Damnit. I did take my name off the mortgage.

"Ok, let me get my supervisor, I will be right back."

The supervisor returns, looks at the account, and states that account is current. He informed me that my name is no longer on the mortgage. I knew he was going to say that. How is the loan current? My heart started racing.

"Excuse me? Wha- Wha- What do you mean?" I began stuttering.

"The loan is current, sir. I'm sorry. I can't provide you with any more information about this account."

"Thank You."

I walked away dazed, confused, not knowing what to think. Maybe Shawna does know what is going on, and she is trying to play me. She took all of our money. Well her money out of the account, which meant she knew about the mortgage being past due. I began feeling sick.

My phone began vibrating. I looked down and it was Shawna.

"Hey baby." I play it cool.

"Hey hun, are you busy? Can you talk?"

"Sure"

"Mr. Johnson says today is my last day. I'll be home late today. Can you pick up TJ from my mom's?"

"Sure."

"I thought you had another week before you got laid off at least?"

"Nope, everyone is packing their things up right now."

"Alright babe, I'll see you when you get home."

Shawna

I followed Terrance to the bank to see what his reaction would be. As I expected he looked like he seen a ghost. I called him just to feel him out. It was true, it was the last day at the office for all of the employee's. I'll show up act like I'm packing my things in case he decides to show up and see if I'm lying.

I walked through the door. Some of the employees looked sad, others looked nonchalant because they were coming with us to the new building. But with some of these severances, nobody should be sad. I head straight for my office and Jamie is sitting in my chair. I have a smirk on my face. I was beginning to look forward to that face when I came into work.

"Well.... Hello." Jamie said. "It's a sad day for some."

"Yep, but a beautiful day for others. Look I have to make it look like I am packing up my things in case my husband stops by."

"You want to talk about it?"

"Nah, in due time. You'll watch everything unfold."

I see Mr. Johnson walking in looking like a million bucks.

"Jamie, Shawna I need to speak with you in private."

"Alright, it's done. The big players are in, here are your checks as promised. I will be in touch in about 2-4 weeks to let you know how everything is going. Within three months we should be back up and running. The employees that we have paid severances to should have enough to cover their expenses for another three months. If not, let me know. We will work something out. We will need them within the next few months to begin prepping everything."

Mr. Johnson looks at me, and asks is everything ok. I nod yes and he winks. I returned to my office. I was going to miss my office.

Current and former employees are coming by office to say their goodbye's, while others are looking uncertain of what is to come. I reassured everyone that is still on board just to hold on and everything will be ok. I knew I couldn't reveal too many details. Jamie returns to my office, and expresses the excitement of opening up our business. I must admit I can't contain my excitement. As I am packing up my things, Jamie makes small talk and begins looking at my family photos.

"You have such a beautiful family, Shawna."

"Why thank you, that's my son TJ and my husband."

"How long have you been married?"

Why is Jamie asking me again?I thought we had this conversation before.

"Well.....uuhhh..... it's been about eight years now, our son is 7, so yep eight years. I lose track sometimes."

"Congratulations, love is such a beautiful thing, so cherish it while you have it."

I noticed Jamie looking at my pictures so intensely.

"Let me go Shawna. We will be in touch I'm sure."

I picked up my pictures and looked at them. We looked so happy. I remember these days even though I was miserable when I was pregnant. I cherished TJ to the fullest, I wouldn't give him up for the world. Terrance and I have been through so much, but these last few months have me questioning our marriage. Are these the game that we are playing? Is he really cheating? My house, our house, what was he thinking? Do I address it? The company? God, I hate keeping secrets. I have to do what is best for TJ and I because I don't know what my so called husband is up to these days.

My cell phone begins ringing snapping me out of my thoughts. I looked down, and while I was thinking of the devil he calls.

"Hello." I say in a flat tone.

"Hey babe, how is everything going?" More importantly, how are you doing?"

"I'm doing fine." I lied.

"How about when you get home, I am going to give you a massage and make dinner for us. I know you have had a long day at work."

"No, I'm ok. I am going to be late coming home today. I have to wrap up some last minute things here at the office with the employees."

"Ok, I'll pick up TJ from your mom's house. We will go from there.

"Thanks honey, love you."

I have noticed that Terrance has been extra nice lately. Since I had my meltdown, he has seemed more eager to help out with TJ and things around the house. I believe he thinks that I am depressed about being laid off. In reality I'm upset about other things that he just has no idea. I wondered am I just as bad as he is, for allowing Jamie to do the things we did at the office with no proof of actual infidelity. I dismissed those thoughts quickly. I had a weak moment. I needed to remember that this man that you have married for better or worse, till death do you part has almost got you evicted from your home, removed his name from the deed of trust, paying a woman money each month from your joint account and skimming money from you. Who is this man I married? I was so deep in my thoughts. I didn't notice Lisa in the doorway.

"Hey Shawna, everything ok?"

"Yea I'm good. I was just thinking that this might be the last time I see this office, that's all."

"Well, look at the bright side. We had a nice run. I hope Mr. Johnson comes through. He did say he would take care of us."

"Yea he did, I mean we are getting a good severance though."

I noticed Lisa making small talk. I wondered what she is digging for.

"What's up?" I asked.

"What's going on Shawna, I'm your girl. You been so intertwined with Terrance these days. I don't get to see you, I just feel like I'm just your assistant these days. Everything good with you?"

"Yeah, I'm good. We will catch up soon, I promise. I have noticed that too that lately I have been shutting everyone out."

"Aight girl, I'll talk to you later."

Was it that obvious, have I been that isolated that I shut everyone out? I don't even talk to my own mother as much because I felt like my needs weren't being fulfilled as a housewife. Was I depressed? Lisa had been my friend since high school. I wondered how long has she been feeling this way.

I finished packing and noticed it was becoming late. I looked down at the time it was 8:48 p.m. I didn't realize that I had been in the office that long. I guess it is time for me to go home and put this show on the road.

Terrance

I noticed the tone in Shawna's voice. She sounded really upset about the news of the lay off. I offered her a massage and dinner. I was going to pick up TJ from my mother-in-law's house. My mother-in-law and I never have really seen eye to eye. She has always felt that I was never good enough for her daughter, even when I have proved myself over and over again. I guess with all the shit I've been doing over the years, maybe I'm not good enough for her daughter. I questioned myself. Ms. Pat always says it's something about you I can't put my finger on. But I don't like you. They say old folks are intuitive. She loves TJ and I can't keep her from her grandson.

Ms. Pat lives in a pretty nice neighborhood. She has had the same home for 30 years and refuses to move even when Shawna offered. I pulled up to Ms. Pat's home, and realized that Jamie has texted me. I sit in the car for a minute before I pick up TJ.

"Hey babe, what are you doing?"

"Picking up my son from my mother in law. What's up?"

"Wanted to see if u wanted to come thru tonight?"

"I'll let you know."

I forgot I left Jamie hanging the other night. Ms. Pat greets me at the car as I am putting my phone away. She was giving me the evil eye.

"Well, how are you Terrance?" She says sarcastically.

"I'm fine, Ms. Pat, and yourself?" I give her a fake smile.

"TJ is in the house. My god I love that boy. He is in with one of my friends Ms. Tina." She was beaming with happiness.

"How was he? He didn't give you any trouble, did he?"

"No, of course not!"

I entered the home, and I was greeted by Ms. Tina. She was an older lady maybe the same age as Ms. Pat. She was a light skinned, shorter lady with long brown hair. I had seen her like once or twice before.

"How are you today ma'am?"

"Oh no!" She laughed. "Don't call me ma'am. Call me Tina. I'm well. You have such a great little boy. He is so intelligent."

"Why, thank you Tina. He is great isn't he?"

It looked like Tina was leaving. She mentioned to Ms. Pat that she was having a cookout this upcoming weekend and should bring her family. Ms. Pat agrees and reminds me to tell Shawna.

"Don't forget Terrance to tell Shawna about the cookout this weekend. She hasn't been returning my calls lately. I don't know what you have done my girl."

I ignored that last statement.

"Have a good day Ms. Pat."

I can't for the life of me understand why she doesn't like me. I didn't really have a mother of my own in my adult life, so it was important for me to gain her acceptance. Which I never did. TJ interrupted my thoughts.

"Daddy, I learned something new today at Grandma's house."

"What's that?" I asked inquisitively.

"Did you know there are 43 presidents?" I feigned ignorance.

"No, TJ I did not know that!"

"Grandma told me and said that President Barack Obama was the first ever black president. But I know he is some part white though, but he looks black."

"Yep, Grandma is right!"

I guess Ms. Pat isn't so bad after all he does love her. It is the only grandmother he has.

I get home a little after 6:00 p.m. and noticed that Shawna still isn't home, so I cooked dinner for us. We watched some cartoons and eat dinner. It was now 8:00 p.m. and I still haven't heard from Shawna. I just assumed that she was just busy with her last day at work and I didn't want to bother her.

I looked down at my phone and noticed a few texts, a few from Tonya, and 2 from Jamie, and 1 from Dana. The texts from Tonya reads:

6:05 p.m. - "What's up? So you just going to ignore me now like we were never together?"

6:13 p.m. - "Why are you doing this to me?"

6: 22 p.m. - "Well I need some money, so if you really don't want me to tell your wife, you need to come up off some money."

6:48 p.m. - "I'm sorry, I didn't mean to threaten you, I'm sorry. I just want you to talk to me Terrance."

I ignored all of her texts. I am going to have to do something about her. I was going to text her later. I read my texts from Jamie and a little smile comes across my face. I swear Jamie makes me feel some type of way that Shawna doesn't even make me feel. I don't know if it was the sex or what. I really don't know Jamie like that, so I don't know what I am feeling.

6:25 p.m. "Hey, what's going on?"

6:50 p.m. "Well I'm going to take that as a no, since I haven't heard from you yet."

I texted Jamie back:

"Just waiting on some things to come through. I will text you later on tonight."

I'm moving through text messages. This was getting tiresome now. Dana texted me:

6:35 p.m. "Hey daddy, I miss you, come through."

I ignored that text, and wait for Jamie to text me back. I'll probably just tell Shawna I am going to the gym tonight so I can meet up with Jamie. I put my phone down and start watching T.V. with TJ again when I hear the door open. Shawna comes in. She looks like she has had a long day. I meet her at the door, grab her things from her, and kiss her.

"How was your day, babe?" She snaps!

"How was my day? How the fuck do you think my day was? I was just laid off today from my job!"

"Babe, sssshhh TJ is in the living room."

"I'm sorry, I'm having a rough day." She starts crying.

I give her a hug something I haven't done with my wife in a long time. I noticed how warm it felt. She starts crying harder.

"Babe, it will be ok. You will find something. You have the experience and education to work at any of these major corporations in the city."

"That's not the point Terrance, I wanted to go back to work at this job, not another one!" She was sobbing.

"I'll tell you what I am going to run you a bath, and just take some time to yourself. I will stay out here with TJ. I will put him to bed soon."

Shawna didn't even acknowledge anything I just said. She just left the room and went upstairs. I noticed my wife needed me. She needed me more now than anything. I texted Jamie and say I'll be late coming over tonight. I put TJ to bed and realize that he looks so innocent. If I don't stop my ways, I am going to lose my family and everything. I finally realized that it isn't about money, it's about my family. I guess growing up with a hard life made me hard. I didn't realize what was really important was my family and not money. For the first time in years, I look at my wife. I mean really looked at my wife. I look at how stunning she is. She is the mother of my son, my only son, she was the leader in one of the top investment firms in the city. She is independent. She has made sacrifices that I didn't expect her to and she still stood by my side. I'm still complaining. What the fuck is wrong with you Terrance? Maybe I was fucked up in the head.

"Hey, how do you feel?"

"Better, a lot better."

"Oh yeah. Your mom's friend invited us to a cookout this weekend. She wants us to bring TJ. I thought it would be nice if we go."

"That's fine, we can go."

I didn't know what else to say. I watched her get out of the tub, put on her robe, and lotions herself down. Then she gets in the bed. I get in the shower after she does and I get out of the shower and realized that Shawna is asleep. I texted Shawna and tell her I was going to the gym and will be back later.

I texted Jamie:

"I'm on my way but I can't stay long."

I pulled up to Jamie's house and knock. Jamie greets me fully clothed.

"I thought you weren't coming."

"I texted you and told you I was."

"Oh...... well I was about to head out to my mom's house. We are going to have to do this another time."

"No, we not." I was a little aggressive.

I pushed Jamie back in the door way and grab Jamie gently, and began licking Jamie's neck.

"I want a chance to make things up from last time, as I was gently massaging Jamie's ass."

I throw Jamie down on the bed, and begin stripping Jamie's clothes off.

"Turn over."

"I like it when you're rough, Terrance!"

"Oh, you do!"

I slide in gently, but then start going harder and and then slower. I noticed Jamie screaming in ecstasy as I saw Jamie playing with my balls. Jamie's ass looked so good from behind. After about 15 minutes of non-stop fucking I cum.

"Damn, Terrance that was good! You definitely made up for last time!"

"I did, didn't I!" I was feeling myself and out of breath.

Jamie climbs on top.

"Uh, uh, I can't go again, not right now." I was still panting.

Jamie begins kissing all on my neck. My dick begins to get hard again. What the fuck? I never get hard again this fast.

"Hmmmm." Jamie begins circling the head of my dick.

"Damn." Then my dick gets soft again.

"It's ok, I gotta go anyway. I'm going to jump in the shower."

"Can I join? I didn't know what has come over me lately with Jamie. Was I craving some type of other attention? I haven't even felt this way with anyone that I was just fucking, maybe Tonya. But that was different. We start talking while we in the shower.

"Tell me why a man like you isn't with anybody? You said you had a son. Where is the mother?"

"I really don't like to talk about my personal life upfront, but yeah I got a son."

"It's cool, well maybe we can get to know each other a little more over time."

We both get out the shower. I was wondering why Jamie was asking personal questions now. Was Jamie feeling me too? I couldn't think about this shit right now. I leave thinking about Jamie. It is something about Jamie. My mind was wondering. I just said I needed to be a better man and here I am just leaving Jamie's house. I return back to my house. I take my keys and phone out of my pocket and sit it on the nightstand. I crawled up next to Shawna, it was a little after midnight. I was exhausted.

Jamie

Today was kind of stressful to say the least. But seeing Shawna today kind of turned me on. I took a good look at her family pictures today and realized that I was fucking her husband. I played it off and started asking about her family. I returned to my office to finish packing. My mother calls, she had been calling all day. I finally answered.

"Hey Jamie, what are you doing?"

"Nothing mom, what's going on?"

"Remember, I'm having a family gathering this weekend, your sister will be there."

"I will be there I can't wait to have your macaroni and cheese."

"Alright, Jamie I will see you soon."

My sister and I haven't seen each other in years, it'll be nice to see her. I think it's been about five or six years now. We don't talk at all. The last time I think I talked to her she had just gotten married and invited me to the wedding. I didn't attend because I was out of the country. We haven't seen eye to eye since. Mom told me she is divorced now. I loved my sister. We just never seen eye to eye when it came to men. I just wanted the best for her.

I texted Terrance to see if he wanted to meet up tonight, I already knew he was married even though he didn't tell me.

I wanted to see how much of a dog he really was. Maybe I was horny or maybe I just didn't really care. Whatever my reasoning was, I still wanted to text him. Before you go judging me, I am not the one married here. I can do what I want and who I want. He did tell me he had a son, something he didn't tell me before. He is giving me personal information about his whereabouts. I wondered if he is trying to get to know me better. I never got a response from Terrance, so I call my mom back. I told my mom that I would be coming over later tonight to help her cook. Terrance popped up at my home saying he texted me. He was a little more aggressive this time.

I can definitely say that Terrance made up for the other night. He was definitely on point. I couldn't help but to reminisce about that dick. I hope I am not falling for an ain't shit man that is already married. If you ask me both of them ain't shit. We had a bit of an intimate moment in the shower, when Terrance asked could he join me in the shower. I was shocked but I enjoyed every minute of it.

I pulled up to my mom's house. She is such an awesome lady. But me and my mom have never seen eye to eye. She is just doing what a mother does and that is protect me. I guess me and her are alike in some ways. But sometimes she can be a little overprotective. That led her to push me and my sister away. I never looked back. I knocked on the door.

"Hey mom." I said dryly.

"JJJJAAAAMMMMIIIIIEEEE!!!!"

She is hugging me like she hasn't seen me in forever, wait it has kind of been forever. It's been about five years now I think. I swear she is trying to cut my oxygen off because she was hugging me so tight.

"I missed you so much Jamie. I can't believe you are really here!"

"Yes, mom I'm here."

"Come in the kitchen with me, I'm just cooking some meatballs now. I know we haven't been in touch lately and Jamie I want you to know I'm sorry. I never meant to hurt you or your sister."

"Mom it's ok. I'm sorry because I haven't been in touch. I shouldn't have let our disagreements come between our relationship. You are still my mother."

"No, no, I was being so judgmental of your lifestyle that I pushed you away. I shouldn't have done that. You deserve my support and I deserve grandbabies." She laughed.

"I don't know about the grandbabies part yet mom. But I'm working on it." I lied.

We finished cooking some of the other food. I noticed that my mother and I had such a good time cooking and catching up. I realized that I only have one mother. I can't do this to her again.

I went into my old room, she has kept it the same. I laid in my bed, and wondered how did I even get to this point in my life. I wanted to settle down. I wanted to stop sleeping around. I wanted someone that will love me for me and not my money. Mom is talking grandbabies, I don't know if I am ready for that yet. Shit, I think I'm too selfish for children.

I woke up to this aroma in the house something I haven't smelt in years, pancakes, some type of pork, maybe bacon or sausage, and something else. I rushed out of the bedroom because I wanted to see what my mom was cooking. It was everything I thought and more. There were pancakes, bacon, sausage, eggs, fried potatoes, toast and fried fish. My mom was cooking as if she would never see me again.

"Mom, why are you cooking so much food?"

"Your sister said she was on the way over so I made extra for her too."

"Wow! I haven't seen her in forever either."

As I sat down to eat, I heard a knock at the door. My mom goes to the door and I heard some voices. it sounded like my sister, but I couldn't tell. She comes around the corner. It was her in the flesh.

"Hey sis, how are you?" I started to become teary eyed.

"I'm good. I missed you Jamie!"

We hug for a long time and it felt like minutes until mom interrupted us.

"Look at all this food mom made us!"

"We haven't eaten like this since we were kids!" she says.

"I know! I can't wait!"

Mom disappears and returns fully dressed saying she has to go the store to pick up a few last minute things. My sister and I started talking.

"What have you been up to sis?"

"Nothing much." She avoids eye contact.

"C'mon sis, what's going on? I know when something is wrong."

"Jamie, you don't know me! Why you want to be all up in my business now?" she snapped.

"I'm sorry, I just know when something is wrong that's all."

"Well it's…. umm…. I met this guy, and everything was cool. He was, I mean is a great guy, nice job, good to me, pays for everything. We had been messing around for a while, then all of a sudden he cuts me off."

"What? Why? I asked?"

"I don't know Jamie. He said that he didn't want to anything to do with me anymore so he cut me off. I mean he was paying all of my bills everything Jamie. He was great!" She was talking so fast, but something didn't make sense.

"Maybe we had someone else sis. Do you think that's why he didn't want to commit to you?"

She does it again, looks down as if she was ashamed.

"What?"

"Well…. ummm….. he is kinda committed to someone else."

"Oh no! Sis don't tell me he's married?"

"Yeah, but I thought he was going to leave his wife!"

"Did he say he was going to leave his wife?"

"No…. but I thought he was. We even talked about it."

"Sis, I have told you about messing with these married men!"

"C'mon Jamie like you are any better. How many married people have you messed with?"

"We aren't talking about me. We are talking about you!"

"You need to get pass this guy. He doesn't deserve anyone like you, especially if he is putting you down like that. He doesn't respect!"

"I know. I know. But it is nice to vent about it."

"You know I am always here if you need to talk. Let's get ready for this cookout, I can't wait to eat, drink and dance. You remember how we used to cut up!"

"Yea, I remember!"

It was nice talking to my sister, she was *always* going through something. We both deserved better. She deserved better. I can't wait until we both can get it together.

Shawna

I woke up to Terrance cuddled under me, it was still dark. I looked at the clock and its 4:11a.m. I moved from under him because I had to go to the bathroom. I saw Terrance's phone light up. I glanced at the clock again, thinking it might be work related. He usually doesn't have his phone out in plain sight. I check his phone and see 17 messages from Tonya, 2 messages from James and 3 messages from Damien. I wanted to check the messages but I didn't want to make it seem like I didn't trust him. As I was contemplating on checking the messages, another message comes through from Tonya and says:

"Baby, I am sorry for all the messages. I am just really upset that you won't talk to me, and it has been a really long time since I've seen you. Can you just call me so we can straighten all of this out?"

Everything I have ever thought just came flooding to my mind. Was he really cheating? This message says at least he has been seeing her. Is this the same Tonya he was writing checks to, giving money to? I was wide awake now. I was looming over him, looking at him confused. I felt like I could kill him in his sleep. First the business, the house and now this. It was almost as if my world has come crashing down on me all at once. I laid in bed ruminating in my thoughts. I didn't know who to turn to, who to call because I have shut almost everyone out. Maybe I could call Jamie tomorrow. Jamie has been the closet things to a friend that I have right now. I tried to go back to sleep, but I just tossed and turned to the point of waking Terrance up.

"Babe, what's wrong?" He asks sleepily.

"Who is Tonya?" I cut straight to the point.

"Huh, what?" He looks confused, then confusion turned to what looked like worry.

"You heard me. Who is Tonya?"

"Who?"

"Don't play with me Terrance! You have 1.5 seconds to tell me who Tonya is before I'm on an episode of snapped!"

"Um, babe Tonya is just a friend from work."

"We have friends now? Friends from work that I don't know about? Friends from work that text you 4 in the morning? Get the fuck out of here Terrance with that bullshit!" I was yelling.

"You went through my phone Shawna!"

"Oh no! Don't try to turn this shit on me Terrance. I woke up to go to the bathroom and your phone was blowing up!" I lied. "I thought it might be work so I looked at it and I see a text from Tonya!"

"You know what Shawna, I'm not doing this shit right now, with TJ in the house. We are not doing this!"

"Oh yeah! So you're going to Tonya house now? Is there where you going? I know about the house Terrance! I know you didn't pay the mortgage! I know you removed your name from the deed of trust! I know about the company Terrance, I *know* everything! I know you have been writing Tonya checks! I know you have been skimming money from me! I know it all!"

I blew up. I no longer could play this little game with him. Terrance looked like he had seen a ghost. All the blood drained from his face, like he was trying to think of his next move.

"Now tell me what the fuck is going on?" I heard the doorbell ring, it must be Lisa. I called Lisa to come get TJ and take him to my mom's house so we could finish this argument alone. I know Terrance head was spinning, so was mines.

"Hey girl, here is TJ's bag with his toys tell my mom I will call her in a little while. Thank you so much!"

"No problem, I'll see you later." Lisa said.

I waited for Lisa and TJ to leave, then I begin going off again.

"You better have something to say Terrance because shit is about to hit the fan real fucking quick!"

"Babe, baby, look I wanted to tell you the truth but I know you can't handle it right now!"

"Terrance, I am tired of your stupid games. If you don't tell me you can get the hell out of *my* house. I will be ok without you!"

"Alright, Shawna you wanna know? You really wanna know! Fine I'll tell you! I fucked you over with the company because Mr. Johnson company was going under anyway so I was doing it for us. Tonya… well Tonya was a chick I was fucking for a minute. I was paying her to keep quiet. This was around the time I thought we were going to divorce. The money thing, I knew if we divorced and you weren't working, you would take half of everything. That's why I did it! You happy!" He blew up.

The tears flooded my eyes, I couldn't believe what the fuck I was hearing. I had to compose my thoughts to believe that my husband of all these years would do this to me. He has been fucking with Tonya when we were about to get a divorce, that was some years ago. She was still around. Was our marriage that fucked up he couldn't tell me about our business?

"If you want me to leave I will. I will understand."

"No, no, stay! We are going to talk about this shit! There is obviously some things wrong in our marriage that I didn't know was wrong. Enlighten me Terrance what was so wrong in our marriage that you felt like you had to lie, cheat and steal from me? From me, your own wife? When we were going to get a divorce that was a few years ago Terrance? Or were you planning on divorcing me recently? You're telling me that this bitch has been around for a few years? Were you going to leave me for this bitch?"

I was firing questions back to back.

"Shawna, you know I came from a hard life. When things got rocky between us a few years ago I wanted to protect me. Then a few months ago yea I was thinking about divorce then too. Shit was rough Shawna. I didn't know how much more I could take. You were depressed, you neglected me, you isolated yourself. Instead of being there as a man for you and not understanding what you were going through. I left you to deal with it on your own and for that I apologize. I was selfish, and ignorant. I want you to know I know now what is important and it's not money, it's my family. Tonya, has been around for a few years. You are the mother of my child, my wife, what has kept this family together. It took me to see you down this time after being laid off to realize that. I am sorry I know it will take a lifetime to make it up but I am sorry. Please forgive me, and everything I've done. I know it's asking a lot but please, please forgive me." I was begging. I was trying to only answer the questions she asked me, nothing more.

This man was begging, something I've never seen Terrance do in my life. But boy was he laying it on thick. Who was this man I married? I didn't know if he was sincere, or he was plotting. I looked at him with disgust, and absolute shame.

"You know what, this has shown me what type of person you are. Terrance, not only are you the worst type of man, you are the worse type of husband. I don't know if I can ever forgive you for this."

We didn't talk for hours. I was upstairs, he was downstairs. I really wanted to get out of the house, so I go downstairs.

Terrance looked like he had lost his best friend. He was sitting in the dark looking at the wall.

"We will go to my mom's friend cookout today and we will have a good time. TJ is going to be staying at my mom's for the weekend. You better be on your best behavior until I say everything is good!"

"Ok."

Terrance

Shawna was tossing and turning, I wonder what was bothering her so much. I turned over to look at my phone it was 7:38 a.m. I was thinking I might as well wake up. But why did I do that? Shawna got straight to the point.

"Who is Tonya?"

My face tightened up, I was worried. I had to think quick but she caught me off guard. I thought I would be prepared better than this and I wasn't.

"She is a work friend." I lied.

I know I had to come better than that, but I wanted to figure out how much Shawna knew before I gave her more details.

"So we have friend now? Friends that we work with? Friends that I don't know about? That text you 4 in the morning?"

Damn it Tonya! Why did you have to text me? This crazy stalker bitch is really humming on my nerves now. I usually have my phone face down but this particular day, I didn't because I was tired. Jamie got me moving sloppy. Then Lisa comes to the door. My head was spinning because Lisa hasn't been to the house in a long time. As far as I knew, her and Lisa weren't friends anymore. Lisa was the one that tried to convince her not to marry me. When she came to get TJ, I had a confused look on my face. Shawna began to tell me she knew everything, about the company, the money, the house and Tonya. She asked me was I going to leave her for Tonya. I had to lie. She would have left me for real. My heart was beating so fast I just knew for sure she was going to leave me. All I could think about is how I fucked up and I don't know how I was going to make it right so I began begging. I hoped it work.

She goes upstairs. I sit downstairs for what seemed like a few hours. I contemplate my next move since she knows everything. I was upset to say the least. I was sitting in the dark. I thought I would have been better prepared. Through all of this I still couldn't get my mind off Jamie.

"We will talk more about this later I am looking forward to going to this cookout." she says.

All I can think about is the bullet I dodge knowing that this was going to be put on hold for a while until I can come up with how to smooth this over. Terrance, you have fucked up big time and I have a feeling it's just the beginning. I'm getting ready to go to this cookout. I noticed that Shawna continues to give me the evil eye. It's a look that I've never seen before, almost a look of hatred. I feel so bad deep down and I don't know how to fix it. Should I have lied? Why did I have to tell the truth? I still lied in telling the truth. I'm kidding myself, the lies are what got me in the position in the first place. I'm glad that she doesn't know about Jamie, or Dana. She would really flip if she knew it was more than one. I put their names as James and Damien in my phone. Why I didn't do that for Tonya? I got too comfortable. If she knew I was going to leave her for Tonya, I think I'll be dead for real. One may be forgivable, but two more I think she would literally have my head. I had it all how could I do this to her, all because of my selfishness. I stand to lose my whole family.

Shawna

God, I hate that man at this very moment. I can't even think straight right now. My blood was still boiling. I needed to go to the cookout and have a few drinks so that I could temporarily get away from all of this. I texted Lisa:

"Hey, how is TJ doing?"

Then I scrolled through my contacts and I looked at Jamie's name. I contemplated on texting Jamie. My panties got wet just thinking about it. It's temporary. So, I texted Jamie:

"Hey, Jamie how are you?"

Immediately, Jamie responded back:

"I'm good, everything ok?"

I started to think about whether or not I should tell Jamie my personal business. We are about to business partners. He will find out eventually.

"No everything isn't ok; I feel like everything around me is falling apart."

"Can you talk?"

"Not right now."

"How about this my people is having something like a family reunion this evening. Jow about you swing by and meet my family to get your mind off things?"

"No, I can't, I have other plans this evening, thank you for the invite though."

I really wanted to take Jamie up on the invite just to get away from Terrance. But we had already committed to attending this one.

Lisa texted me back:

"TJ is great, he is such a good kid!"

That made my heart happy. He was the one thing that made me happy at this moment. He was innocent in all of this even if his daddy was an ass.

✳✳✳

We arrived at my mother's house to pick up TJ. We were all taking one car, since it would be easier that way. My mom has this friend Ms. Tina, she is such a wonderful lady from what I can tell. I've only met her only once or twice. But she is a godsend since my father passed away. She has really been there for my mom even when I wasn't.

"Shawna, is that you?" As my mom approaches the car.

"It's me, mom." She gives me a warm hug, something I really needed. She hugged me extra long, almost like she knew I needed it.

"Are you ready?"

"Yep, we are ready let me grab my jacket and we can be on our way."

The car ride was quiet, except TJ humming to the music in the car. My mom didn't like Terrance, she always said it was something about him she didn't like. Maybe I should have listened to her, Lisa and everyone else. Maybe I wouldn't be in this situation. We pulled up to Ms. Tina's house and there are lots of people. I didn't know any of them. I was going to just stick with my mom and Terrance the entire time because they were my comfort zone. We maneuver through the crowd and find seating on the outside patio. Terrance tries to make small talk.

"You want anything to drink or food?"

"Yes, can you get me a beer?"

"Yea, babe sure."

I looked around and did not see anyone I knew. This woman sits next to me, and tries to talk to me.

"Hey, how are you doing?"

"I'm ok." I was annoyed.

"It's a nice turn out. Don't you think?"

"Yea it is."

"So how do you know Ms. Tina?"

Before I answered I thought this lady was asking too many questions. Maybe she was trying to get to know me. I smiled and continued to talk to her.

"Her mother and my mother are good friends. She invited me and my husband to the cookout."

"Oh wow, is Ms. Pat your mom? I didn't know that! Ms. Tina is my mom, small world huh?"

Terrance returned with my beer. he looked agitated like someone has pissed him off. Then again, we did have an argument before we left. I observed the lady get up and introduces herself. I didn't catch her name, but Terrance seemed a bit standoffish.

"Everything ok?"

"Yea everything is fine."

I noticed a shift in Terrance almost an anxiousness. I couldn't explain it. I was here to have a good time even if I didn't know anybody.

Jamie

The cookout had started and everyone began pouring in. People I haven't seen since I was a kid, or at least within the last ten years. I mingle a little. I saw some unfamiliar faces. I greeted them too. My sister comes over and makes small talk. She confesses to me that she was still texting that guy that was married.

"Why are you putting yourself through this?"

"I just want him to talk to me Jamie. Is that so wrong?"

"Yes, because you are humiliating yourself."

My sister acted like she seen a ghost.

"What's wrong?"

"You remember that guy I was telling you about?"

"Yea…."

"He just walked out to the patio with his wife."

"He is here. How does he know mom? I don't understand. Did you invite him or something?"

"No! Why would I invite him Jamie? He has never even met mom."

As I get ready to turn around, mom calls me.

"Jamie, can you help me take some of this food outside?"

Tonya disappeared. I wondered what that was about. I hope she doesn't go and do anything crazy. As I was helping mom take the food outside, I turned around and bumped into Terrance. I was shocked that he was there. What the fuck was he doing here? My mom immediately greeted him.

"Hey Terrance, how are you doing baby? I'm glad you could make it. Where is your wife?"

"She is sitting on the patio. I was going to bring her a beer."

"Since you're here, can you help Jamie bring some of the food outside?"

"Sure."

My head was spinning. Terrance was here with Shawna and knew my mom. What have I gotten myself into? I played it cool. I didn't want my mom in my business. As I am bringing the food outside, I noticed Tonya talking to Shawna. The thoughts begin to flood my mind. Why is Tonya talking to Shawna? Do they know each other? I noticed Terrance go over and gives Shawna her beer. I noticed his face become tight as Tonya greets him. Tonya begins walking towards me.

"What's that all about?" I asked her.

"Oh nothing, I was just talking to Shawna."

"Do you know her?"

"Not really….kinda." She shrugged her shoulders.

I noticed a look in Tonya's eye like she was up to something.

"C'mon Tonya spit it out."

"You know that guy I was telling you about that was here with his wife?"

My heart was racing. Please do not tell me it's Terrance. Please don't tell me it's Terrance.

"He is sitting over there with his wife. I just went to make small talk."

"What? So that's the guy?"

"Yep, he is fine. Isn't he?"

"Yea, he is." I agreed as Terrance and I were making unknown eye contact.

"Tonya, why are you being messy in talking to his wife? That is petty."

"I know. I wanted to see the look on Terrance's face when he saw me talking to his wife."

"What did he say?"

"Nothing, he just said hi."

Tonya walked off seeming satisfied with what she just did. I was feeling like my heart is going to beat out of my chest. I felt sick. Me and my sister were fucking the same guy? And I did some freaky shit with his wife. This world is too small. I knew I shouldn't have come home. This is about to get messy. Tonya was up to something I just know it. I wanted to leave.

Tonya said they had been messing around for a few years now. I mean I can't blame Terrance for fucking her. I mean me and my sister got it going on. I was so taken aback with everything that was going on, I didn't realize that my mother had snuck up behind me.

"Jamie, why aren't you eating?"

"I am going to eat, I am not feeling well right now. I'm going to lay down for a little bit. I'll be back."

I went back into the house. Everything was such a blur. I wanted to throw up. I've been known to be messy, but not this messy. Don't get me wrong, I have messed with my share of married men, but never men that my sister has messed with. I bumped into Shawna on the way back to my room, as she was coming out of the bathroom.

"Hey Shawna, everything ok?"

She looked like she had been crying because her eyes were all red and swollen.

"I'm ok, Jamie thanks for asking."

"Are you sure?"

"No, I'm not. Is there somewhere we can talk privately?"

I directed Shawna to my old room. She began telling me everything about Terrance, about Tonya, about the company. Luckily, she doesn't know about me. All I could think was this man is a dog. Shawna didn't know that Tonya is my sister, so this could turn really bad. Apparently, she doesn't know what Tonya looks like either.

"I'm sorry Jamie to involve you in my drama."

"No, no Shawna it's ok, I can't believe all that he has done. I am here for you whenever you need to talk."

Shawna and I walked out the bedroom. We ran straight into Terrance. Terrance looked like he had seen a ghost and looked between me and Shawna. Shawna speaks up first.

"Uh….Hi Terrance, um Terrance this is Jamie a former co-worker of mines."

He shakes my hand.

"Nice to meet you Jamie."

"Nice to meet you too." As we have unknown exchange.

Shawna and Terrance walked away. I can't help but to think I dodged a bullet. I wondered what was going on in Terrance's mind.

"Jamie!" Tonya says.

"What?" she startled me.

"Why are you looking at them like that? I saw you talking to Shawna you know her?"

"Yea, she is a former co-worker of mines."

"I didn't know that, what a small world." Then she walks off.

A really small world.

Terrance

I thought I was about to shit on myself when I saw Jamie. What the fuck was going on? I had to play it cool because it was a family function. I pretended like I didn't know Jamie. Then as my day could get any fucking worse, I see Tonya talking to Shawna. I had to play that cool like I didn't know her. The inside of me wanted to just cuss her out. Why is she here? Was she stalking me? Shawna looked unbothered by the fact this unknown woman was talking to her. I know she was still pissed off.

"Hi, I'm Tonya."

"Hello." I said to Tonya. If looks could kill.

Tonya looks like she has this devilish look in her eye, almost as if she was up to something. I didn't like it at all. I knew if I snapped, she would blow my shit, so I tried to play it cool as possible. The only thing I had going for me was that Shawna didn't know what Tonya looked like. I wondered what was Jamie doing here too. Why is Tonya here too? It didn't make sense. Does Jamie and Tonya know each other? Shawna interrupted my thoughts.

"What's wrong with you?" Shawna asked.

"Nothing."

Yea, ok." I saw your face get tight when I was talking to her. You fucking her too?"

"No, Shawna I'm not." I lied. My face got tight.

I get up and walked off, because I couldn't do this with Shawna right now. I had to think of my next move which was to leave. If she keeps pissing me off, I might leave for real. I go out to my car because we parked two streets over. I needed a breather before I snapped. Maybe I can convince Shawna to leave early, before whatever Tonya is planning comes to fruition. As I am grabbing for my keys, a person runs up behind me and puts their arms around me. I thought it was Shawna.

"Hmmm, babe that feels so good from you. I thought you were still mad at me."

"I know it does… Terrance." I recognized the voice immediately. I pry her hands from around me.

"What, what the fuck are you doing?" I was looking around nervously to see if anyone saw the exchange.

"You scared your lil' wife is going to see me? I've already introduced myself to her. Where is that cute little boy of yours?"

"Listen, Tonya stay the fuck away from me and my family!" I was pissed, I felt like I was going to blow a gasket. I had lost control of my life.

"You're hurting me Terrance. I like it when you're rough!"

"Tonya, don't play with me. Stay the fuck away from my wife and my son!"

"Terrance why don't you want us anymore?" She says innocently.

"There was never an us, Tonya! NEVER! You wanted to talk so there it is. We were just messing around. Nothing more, nothing less than that!" I was pissed.

"Terrance, I think it was more than that. I think you cared. Why else were you paying my bills? Why else were you checking up on me? Why else were you about to leave your wife for me? Remember?"

She was right. We did talk about it. How could I not think she wouldn't be crazy when I talked about leaving my wife for her. But I'm starting to think this bitch is delusional. Now I really think I may have a serious problem.

"Look Tonya, I need to get back. We are done talking!"

"Terrance... wait!"

I continued to walk off as I am searching for Shawna. She wasn't where I left her. I begin walking around the house, looking for her. I see her coming from Jamie's direction. What the fuck? She knows Jamie too? My heart starts racing, It feels like I'm about to have a heart attack. Jamie and I are making eye contact. I didn't want to draw any attention to myself, so I relaxed a little. Shawna spoke up and introduced Jamie as a former co-worker. I shook Jamie's hand and we headed out. As I looked back I saw Jamie and Tonya talking. How deep is this shit that I have gotten myself into? I needed to get out, and get out fast.

Shawna

Terrance was playing this reverse psychology bullshit with me and think this is a game. He has the wrong one. He walks off, talking about he needs some air. After a few minutes, I get up and actually wanted to talk to him. I see him talking to a woman. The same woman that was talking to me that he said he didn't know. She was hugging on him, and he looked like he was angry. I observed the exchange. I could obviously tell he was pissed. I couldn't watch anymore and I become teary eyed. I tried to find a bathroom and ran into Jamie. I told Jamie everything even the recent exchange with him and the same woman that was talking to me earlier. Jamie agreed with everything I said. I felt better that I talked to Jamie. Jamie always knows the right things to say. I give Jamie a hug. Jamie and I are leaving the bedroom. We bump right into Terrance. Terrance looked like he was still angry. I speak up quickly, and introduce the two. I introduced Jamie as a former co-worker. Terrance face gets tight, I was like here we go. Terrance wants to leave now. I said my good-bye's to my mother whom said that Jamie would take her home and Ms. Tina. The same woman that spoke to earlier reappears. I give her an evil look, if looks could kill. TJ was spending the night at my mom's so we would have this conversation in the car.

"We will be talking about this in the car!" As I said walking ot the car.

We are walking back to the car, and it was silent. Eerily silent. Midway through the car ride. I asked about the lady at the cookout.

"Who was that chick that was talking to me?"

"I don't know, I told you. Here we go with this shit again!"

"Terrance, don't play with me! I saw that little exchange between you and that same girl that was talking to me. What is her name? Because she sure was hugged up all on you and you sure looked like you were angry about it. Is that Tonya?"

He got quiet. His jaws got tight. I know that look. He was about to explode. I braced myself, because it was nothing that he could say to get his self out of this mess.

"Shawna, we are not doing this right now!" He says through his teeth.

"Oh, we are absolutely doing this right now!"

"Yeah Shawna! That was Tonya ok! I didn't know she was going to be there!"

My throat became dry, my heart was in my stomach. I was hoping that he would say something else. I couldn't even speak.

"I don't know why she was there, I don't know if she followed us or what." He said.

This crazy bitch knew who I was and made it a point to introduce herself to me. She better be glad I didn't catch her name. No wonder Terrance face was tight.

"Why did you lie, when I asked you the first time?"

"Because I didn't want to make a scene."

"You know that's Ms. Tina's daughter."

"What? You mean your mom's friend Ms. Tina?"

"So you're telling me you didn't know that?"

"C'mon Shawna give me a little credit. Why would I do the shit close to home? Now it makes sense why she was there."

We pulled up to the house and we had a long talk about everything. He tells me to sit down and begins to tell me everything about Tonya.

"Shawna, I know you don't want to hear any of this. But I am sorry. The best thing I can do right now is be honest with you. I just want you to listen. I told you before Tonya was someone I was just messing with. A few weeks ago, I stopped messing with her, I stopped sending her money and she has been harassing me since. I can show you the messages. I think she is crazy. She has been saying things like she wants to be with me, replace you, you don't deserve me. Shawna, I promise I have been trying to get rid of her and she is just as aggressive as before you seen it today." I was laying it on thick. I wanted to put the blame back on Tonya, so it'll be less heat on me.

I was lost in my thoughts. Any man will say a woman is crazy to get the heat off of him. Why would she come and try to make small talk with me? It was as if she was taunting me. But I saw the sincerity in Terrance's eyes, something I haven't seen since our wedding day. I also saw fear, like his world was falling apart around him. I felt like he was telling me the truth. We talked for hours about various things. Things he felt went wrong. He took a lot of the blame for everything while I blamed myself for refusing to have sex even if I wasn't in the mood.

It seemed like we were headed in the right direction. I suggested a marriage counselor. He was totally against the idea of it, but said that he would consider it. I was satisfied with our conversation. I wanted to do what it takes to make our marriage work and it seemed like he was on board.

****

A month or so later, everything seemed fine after the cookout. Terrance seemed like he was the model husband. He was attentive, honest and involved me in everything. No more late trips to the gym, no more woman's names in his phone. There were some times that were a little sketchy, but I didn't think much of it. I still didn't tell him about the new business. We weren't there yet. It was still this small part of me that didn't fully trust him yet. It was intuition.

Jamie

After the cookout, it had been a while since I had heard from Terrance. He must have been real nervous, scared or both. I wouldn't be surprised at all. If I was him, I would be scared too. In the meantime, Shawna and I have been getting closer, maybe because we are working on this project in getting the company back on board. But these days it seemed like Shawna had been happier, almost like her and Terrance were good. I didn't want to pry but I did want to know. My sister and I have been closer than ever lately. But she has been saying some crazy things lately about Terrance. She says she had been in communication with Terrance. The thoughts continued to flood my mind because Terrance has been texting me on and off for the last month or so saying things like: "I haven't forgot about you." "I've been wrapped up in work." Almost like he is trying to keep me around long enough to smooth things out with Shawna. I knew I had to cut that off, because he was messing with my sister too. I heard my phone go off. I looked down and its Tonya. I answered.

"Hey, Jamie!"

"Hey, what's up?"

"Nothing, I wanted to tell you the good news!"

"What is it?" I say nonchalantly.

"You have to guess!"

"I don't know, Tonya, what?" Now I was annoyed.

"I'm pregnant! Jamie I'm pregnant. The doctor says I'm only 9 weeks along. But I am pregnant! Guess who's the daddy!"

My mouth gets dry and silent, as if this shit could get any worse. I know she is going to say his name.

"It's Terrance, Jamie! It's Terrance baby! Can you believe it? I told you it was meant to be!"

"You think this is the right thing to do right now, I mean the man *is* married?"

"Jamie, what are you suggesting? That I should get rid of it? You are crazy as he is if you think I'm going to get rid of my baby! He should have been more careful!"

"Alright, Tonya. I am just saying don't be surprised if you don't get the reaction that you are looking for from him."

"He is going to be happy. I know he is!"

"Ok, Tonya, I will have to call you back. I am about to walk into a meeting."

I was shaking my head all the way to the conference room. Shit was really about to hit the fan. I wondered how Terrance was going to talk his way out of this one. It was something eerie about my sister lately, like she has become obsessed with wanting Terrance. I can understand why. But I didn't want her to go crazy over him.

I go into my meeting with Shawna and Mr. Johnson. I looked over at Shawna, and I felt so bad for her. She was a good woman with a man that just won't do her right. Is she the woman for me? We have spent a lot of long nights, and a lot of phone calls together.

"Jamie and Shawna, we have done it! We are back on the map. You can call our employees, and let them know when their start date will be. I couldn't have done it without you two. Y'all are a great match for each other, I feel so comfortable leaving this company to you two." Mr. Johnson says.

He looked at us both as if he knew something we didn't know. I begin to see Mr. Johnson get teary eyed.

"Mr. Johnson, it has been an honor to work under you. I can speak for me and Shawna. You have done so much for us personally, emotionally and I must say financially. It's been a blessing."

"Jamie, Shawna I trust that the both of you will run this company right. Shawna, if you choose you can tell your husband if you like. I know he will be livid. But whether he supports you or is livid will reveal the type of man he is." He winked.

"Thank you Mr. Johnson so much for this opportunity." Shawna says.

"I am excited to get back to work."

"I will be in touch with the both of you soon."

Shawna and I begin talking about how happy we are to finally get this thing up and going again. She explains how she can't wait to celebrate. I offer for us to celebrate together. We leave the office and go to this Italian restaurant not to far from the office. We begin to talk

"How's everything going, Shawna?"

"Well, great now since I, I mean *we* have our company."

"That Mr. Johnson is still wise beyond his years. I must admit."

"That he is, I have been working under him for so long, I forget at times."

I was observing Shawna's mannerisms. She seemed a little off. I couldn't put my finger on it, but something seemed a little off about her. I asked her again.

"Everything ok?"

"Well…." she pauses. "I was thinking of something Mr. Johnson was saying today at the meeting. If I choose to tell Terrance about reopening the company, whether he will be livid or happy. Honestly, I think he is going to be livid, because I kept this secret from him."

"Shawna, he should be happy that you are now the owner of a multi-billion-dollar company. He shouldn't be jealous, or angry about it. He should be supportive." I said softly.

"You're right. If he can't be happy, then something is seriously wrong in our marriage, like other shit isn't already wrong."

I didn't pry any further because I didn't want to be nosey. But I noticed Shawna having one too many drinks tonight. I offered to drive her home.

"I don't want to go home Jamie, I want to go home with you." She says, slurring all of her words.

"No, I need to get you home to your husband. Give me your address."

"No! I want to go home with you!" As she starts to feel all on my manhood.

I must admit it felt so good, I haven't had sex with anyone in a long time well except this other person I met a month or so ago named Dana. Dana and I only had sex once, and it was ok. Not something I think I am going to go back to anytime soon.

I let her continue to rub on my dick as I begin kissing on her neck and rubbing her breasts. I lifted her dress and she was so wet that she has soaked through her thongs.

"Wait…. not here. I live right around the corner. Let's go."

I was so horny, I couldn't wait. We get there in about five minutes. We were both so hot and horny. I rip her dress off, and throw her on the couch and begin kissing and licking all over her. She moans in ecstasy. I began licking from her neck, circling around her breasts, down her naval and then down to her pussy. Damn she is so wet. I feel like I should feel bad for fucking another man's wife. But I don't. This is the first time Shawna and I actually are having sex. I get on top of her, and slide it in gently she moans in ecstasy as I can feel her juices running down my dick. I pump harder, she yells louder. I turn her over and hit it from the back as she is throwing it back harder and harder. I could feel her tightening up as she is about to cum. She yells I'm coming. I exploded in her, as we both collapsed.

I wake up to a non-stop buzzing noise. I looked over at Shawna. She was snoring. I glanced at the clock and its 12:16 a.m. I search for the buzzing noise. It was coming from Shawna's phone. It was Terrance. Shawna needed to get home.

"Shawna, Shawna, wake up babe!"

"Huh? Huh, what?"

"It's after midnight, Shawna!"

"Oh shit, I need to get home!"

"Yea…. Terrance just called, by the looks of it he has called like 30 times!"

"I'll smooth that over, I'm worried about him."

We get in my car, and I drive her back to hers.

"That was amazing Jamie."

She kissed me before she gets out the car. On the ride back home I don't know what to think or feel. I felt like Terrance and I were hitting it off. Now I feel like I'm falling for Shawna, what kind of mess have I gotten myself into?

Terrance

Everything was cool with me and Shawna for the last past month or so. She has been going on interviews for other jobs during the day. Today she said she had a meeting with Mr. Johnson, I wondered what that was about. I keep reflecting on everything Brian told me about the new company. Shawna wouldn't keep secrets from me. Would she? I was texting Jamie on and off lately just to keep Jamie in the loop. I definitely didn't want to lose Jamie over the bullshit that we were going through right now. I know, I know, I just got back right with Shawna. But here I was already plotting on Jamie again. I didn't ask Jamie about where he worked because he had told me he worked in banking. I hadn't heard from Tonya in a while except when I got this message today saying:

"We need to talk now Terrance!"

I ignored her message until later that night when I began to get worried about Shawna. It was after 9:00 p.m. She had never gotten home so late before. I began calling and texting her. In between calling and texting her, I called Tonya after TJ fell asleep.

"What's up, Tonya?"

"Nothing!" She says cheerfully. "I have some good news."

"Well….it must be good news for you, because nothing good can come out of your mouth for us."

"I'm pregnant, Terrance!" She says excitedly.

"And what does that mean?" I said sarcastically.

"We are going to be a family, Terrance! The doctor says I'm 9 weeks."

"I don't know why you are telling me, that is not my baby!"

"It is Terrance! Now me and Shawna are going to be sister wives!"

I hung up on her. There was no way. We didn't use a condom all the time. I was trying to remember the last time we had sex because I didn't remember using a condom. Tonya wasn't the type to sleep around, so it might as well could be mines. I couldn't deal with this shit right now. Where the hell was Shawna? At first I was angry, now I'm worried as the time goes by, it's after midnight now. I hear the door unlock and I yank it open before it opens. It was Shawna.

"Hey babe," she says nonchalantly.

"Where have you been?" She smelled like she had been drinking.

"Oh, me, Jamie and Mr. Johnson went out to celebrate!"

"Celebrate about what, Shawna?" I looked confused.

"Our new company, Terrance!" I am now the co-owner of a multi-billion-dollar investment firm in Maryland. The 2nd largest in Maryland.

"Wait…. what Shawna? You've been drinking, you got laid off baby remember?"

"Yea I did, but we were working on another company, because of everything you fucked up, Terrance." She was pointing her finger in my face. "We paid y'all to pull out, now we will never partner with you again! We got the last laugh."

I could tell she had been drinking. Brian was right. Shawna snuck behind my back and has done the unthinkable and outsmarted me. I was angry, I was jealous, but most of all I was impressed. All kinds of thoughts flooded my mind. She may have more money than me. She can do without me. If she finds about the baby, then I am going to have a real shit storm on my hands. I didn't know how to keep that a secret.

"And you know what Terrance, I want a divorce!" She said slurring all of her words.

"Wait a minute baby. You don't know what you're talking about!" I started getting nervous.

"Yes, I do. You have done me wrong time after time after time. I pulled our phone records, you still talking to Tonya. I looked at them before I pulled up. I was a good woman to you Terrance, and you still doing me dirty. I don't want nothing from you."

I felt like my world was falling apart, Tonya was pregnant. Shawna is the owner of a new company that's worth billions, and I won't be entitled to any of it!

"Babe, I will do anything. Let's go to marriage counseling. I am willing to work on anything for you. Tonya called me! I didn't even answer the phone. She texted me! See! I showed her my call log. What do you want me to do?" I lied.

"Change your number Terrance, only give it to the people that are important. That way there are no excuses!"

"Done!"

I noticed that Shawna's hair was kinda messy, and she looked a little rough. Was she cheating? Or was she just drunk? I immediately dismissed those thoughts from my mind. Shawna has done a lot of things, but I don't think she would cheat on me, would she? I found myself questioning Shawna more and more. But with who? She doesn't talk to anyone. Her and Jamie used to work together. But there wasn't anyone else that she could possibly cheat on me with.

Shawna

Today was a monumental day in history with Mr. Johnson, and Jamie. We were now owners of the 2nd largest investment firm in Maryland. Jamie and I went out to celebrate. Let's say I didn't expect to be fucking him at his home. He has a nice home I might add, and was putting it down! I was still mad at Terrance for everything he has done. I felt like I was making everything even between us now by fucking Jamie. But I felt there was more there between us. I don't know what it was. Maybe what I've been neglecting from my own husband? I accidentally fell asleep at Jamie's house, and woke up to a lot of missed calls from Terrance. I'm pretty sure he shitting a brick right now. I had put a trace on Terrance's phone to see who he was talking to. I parked right around the street to check it. I still had a buzz. Low and behold, he was still talking to her. I must admit she hadn't called or texted lately, so it was obvious that something had to occur for her to call. I had made up my mind. I was asking for a divorce.

Terrance yanked open the door before I even get a chance to open it, and begins to grill me about where I've been. I lied. It wasn't a complete lie, but I told him I was with Mr. Johnson, and Jamie celebrating our new company. I knew I needed to start a little argument to get away from him so he would smell the scent of sex on me. I told Terrance I wanted a divorce. He looked so taken aback like I told him someone had died. He began saying he would go to marriage counseling, I told him he needed to change his number. He agreed. That was easier than I thought. Did I really want a divorce or did I just say that to get him off my back? I questioned myself. I took a shower, headed to bed. After the night of fucking I didn't want Terrance bothering me at all. I woke up to Terrance already out of bed cooking breakfast. I needed to go into work but had a major hangover.

"Good Morning sleepyhead."

I had a major hangover, I reminded myself to take something this morning on the way to work.

"Good Morning." I mumbled.

He handed me a plate with eggs, bacon and pancakes. It did look good.

"Babe, I am going to taking TJ to school. You have a good day at work."

"Alright, I see you later."

Well, that is a change. Breakfast? I never mentioned divorce before. First thing on my list is to call a marriage counselor. I checked my phone and wake up to two texts from Jamie:

> **5:45 a.m. "Good morning baby, I hope you enjoyed last night, I can't wait to see you again."**

> **6:30 a.m. "I'll see you at work, oh I brought bagels."**

Just as I was about to text him back I heard a knock at the door.

"Baby I forgot to tell you I changed my number, I am going to text it to you."

"Ok, see you later."

I get dressed, and leave. I couldn't wait to get to work. I leave out the kitchen to my garage. I was backing out, I stopped to make sure my garage closes. A figure knocks on my passenger side window, it was a female. She bends down, and I see it's Tonya. Was she really stalking us? Is she crazy like Terrance says? I rolled down my window agitated.

"Yes?"

"Hey girl, how are you?"

"Can I help you?" I was annoyed.

"Yea, I wanted to stop by. I tried calling Terrance but he changed his number."

"Ok."

"I needed his number to tell him about the doctor appointments."

"Tonya, I don't have time for your foolishness." I put my car in reverse and get ready to back up.

"We gon' be sister wives' girl! I'm pregnant! Little TJ is going to have a brother or sister." She blurts out.

I felt like my whole world was crashing down.

"What?"

"Yea, I'm 9 weeks! Tell Terrance to call me!" As she skips off.

I couldn't take this. We could work through the infidelity, but not this, not a child born outside our marriage.

As I sped off, I couldn't help but to become teary eyed. What did I do to deserve this? Is this punishment for everything that I have done? Is this punishment for not telling Terrance that I had two abortions after TJ? I went through a hard depression after TJ, and didn't want anymore kids. I had some health issues that took away my sex drive and later found out after the two abortions I couldn't have anymore kids. I never told Terrance in fear of how he would feel about it and in fear that he would leave me. All he did while I was pregnant was keep talking about how he wanted another kid. I can't help but to think this is my fault. I should have given Terrance another kid, maybe he wouldn't have gotten her pregnant. Maybe he wouldn't have begun cheating a few years ago if we had another baby. Shawna snap out it, you didn't cheat first, he did. I turned up my gospel music. I will not let this ruin my day. I can't wait to get to work and see Jamie's beautiful face. He brightens my day these days. I know that it's wrong, but Terrance has really fucked up this time. I will handle him when I get home but right now we had a business to run.

Terrance

Shawna got home and wanted a divorce? I thought
everything was good between us. I guess not as good as I
thought it was. I needed to get it together. Now Tonya is
pregnant. Is it mines? We didn't use a condom all the time.
Nine weeks? I needed to convince her to get an abortion
before Shawna found out. I tossed and turned all night,
wondering how did I get myself in this situation, things
could be much worse I thought. She could have found out
about Jamie, or Dana but she hasn't. I woke up early to
cook TJ and Shawna breakfast. I wanted to show her that I
am changing. I didn't want to go to marriage counseling.
Truth is, I was scared that it will bring up some unresolved
issues that I am not ready to face yet. I know you think I'm
gay or on the DL. I'm not either! Or was I? I'm afraid to
confront my own fears. But if it will save my marriage I am
all about it. My phone starts going off. I look down it's a
text from Dana:

"Hey daddy I miss you! Come thru soon."

I ignored the text. Dana had been texting me a lot lately and
I can't understand for the life of me why I keep dealing
with Dana. I only kept dealing with Dana because I may
need him. I picked up my phone and begin to text Jamie,
wait Jamie didn't have my new number. I didn't have to
worry about either one of them now. For the first time, I
felt calm and not worried. I think Shawna and I can work
on our marriage. I take out my phone to text Shawna.

**"Hey babe, I hope you have a good day at work.
I love you."**

It felt good send that text. I felt like was doing everything
to make it work. Now what to do about Tonya, she knows
where we live. I'm sure she will pop up soon. I sit and
contemplate my next move until Brian comes in my office.

"What's up man?"

"Nothing, sitting here thinking."

"Everything good, with you and Shawna?"

I get up to close my door.

"Shit is bad, real bad. I mean Shawna says she willing to
work things out, but I don't know."

"What did you do man?"

Brian didn't know about the cookout, the arguments or
anything. When we were at work it was about business. We
didn't talk about personal life too much. I had to be careful
what I told Brian. Brian has been with his long time
girlfriend Lisa which is Shawna's best friend. Brian has
proven to be loyal to me even with all the dirt I've done. I
gave Brian all the details, the cookout, the arguments, the
pregnancy, everything. Brian sat down.

"What the entire fuck? How the hell is Shawna still with
you and hasn't cut your dick off?"

"I don't know, I changed my number today. She wanted me
to, so I did."

"What's worse Brian, she came home last night still drunk from celebrating with Mr. Johnson and her new co-owner of her new multi-billion-dollar company. She has been keeping some secrets of her own too. They got the company back up off the ground."

"I told you Terrance! I told you!"

"She asked for a divorce last night. I agreed to go to marriage counseling, and changed my number. It seemed like divorce was off the table for now."

I was interrupted by my secretary,

"Mr. James, you have a visitor here to see you."

"Who is it?"

"A Ms. Billard sir."

"Thank you. I'll be right out."

"Oh shit man, Tonya is here. This chick is crazy. How could I think she wouldn't show up at my job?"

"Try not to make a scene." He walked out of my office.

As I was walking to the front, all I could think was Tonya is becoming a pain in my ass. I see Tonya sitting there smiling from ear to ear.

"Come with me." I look around nervously. I take her into one of our conference rooms.

"Tonya, what the fuck are you doing at my job?" I said in a low whisper, but loud enough to make a point.

"You changed your number. Did you forget I know where you work?"

"What do you want?" I asked agitated.

"Well…. here." She shoves a card in front of my face.

"What is this?"

"It's my next doctor appointment. I want you to be there."

"Look, Tonya are you sure that you want to go through with this? I won't be the father that you want me to be." I was trying to get her to understand that I am not raising this baby with her, but in a nice way.

"Of course, Terrance! What are you saying, you don't want our baby? You want me to get rid of it? Well, newsflash Terrance, I'm not! I saw your wife this morning. I told her we are going to be sister wives!"

My jaw tightened, and I blew up and put my hand around her neck.

"You did what!"

I let go quickly, I was trying not to cause a scene.

She smiled, and said it again.

"Yeah, your wife knows that TJ is going to have a little brother or sister now. No getting rid of me now." She said with a devilish grin.

All I could think about is how Shawna hasn't called me by now to rip my head off. I am liable to come home and all my shit will be sitting in the front yard. This bitch is crazy after all

"Get the fuck out of my office Tonya, NOW!"

"Ok, Terrance but you know you can't get rid of me. You never will!"

My mind was racing. I think I might need to call in some favors. I really didn't want to, as a matter of fact I left those problems along time ago. Now I was desperate, Shawna knows. I don't think our marriage can survive this, not a baby.

I was walking back to my office. Brian caught up with me.

"What was that all about man?"

"Tonya, crazy ass man." I whispered.

We get back in my office and I closed the door.

"She told Shawna that she was pregnant with my baby!"

"Whhhaaaatttt!"

"Yeah man, I don't know what to do. Shawna hasn't called me yet. I don't know what is going on right now. I think I might need to call in a favor man."

"You sure you want to do that Terrance. We have come a long way from home and we been clean since."

"I'm not getting my hands dirty. But I need to make sure she doesn't have the baby."

157

"That's still getting your hands dirty. She still going to be a problem with or without the baby."

"I can handle her without the baby. I think I'm going to call Eddie."

"Alright man just be careful ok. Put some thought into it."

Brian walked out. I had my mind made up midway through conversation.

Edward Toler, we go way back. I'm not sure if he still gets his hands dirty, but he owes me a few favors. Even if he doesn't, I am sure he knows someone who will. You never know what a desperate man will do in a desperate time. I scroll down to his name and I look at it for a long time. Do I need to be man and face my mistakes, or do I need to take care of them? I dialed Eddie.

"Hey Eddie."

"How can I help you today Terrance?"

He knew we were not on business terms in relations to my son, and that it was personal just by the informality.

"I need a favor Eddie."

"Wait a minute. Let me close my door Terrance."

As I sit waiting. I was still contemplating my decision to do this. I was so desperate for my marriage to work. I was willing to go extreme measures.

"What's going on Terrance?"

"Can you meet me for lunch in an hour?"

"Sure. I will text you a location."

I agreed to meet Eddie at this Mexican restaurant downtown. Eddie had aged, but still looked sharp as ever. I look at Eddie as a mentor, almost like a father figure and we were always there for one another whenever we needed it. We may have had our issues with TJ at school, but it was all business.

"Hey Terrance, my man. What do I owe this special occasion?"

"I need a favor Eddie, a favor that needs to go away."

"What is going on? I ain't never seen you like this before, you look desperate."

"I am, Eddie, I am. It's this woman that says she is pregnant with my baby. I need you to make sure she doesn't have it. Don't hurt her, but make sure she doesn't have the baby." I said in a whisper.

"You know I don't get my hands dirty like that anymore, but I know some people. You know it's going to cost you."

"Yea I know, how much?"

"25,000."

"I got you. What do you need from me?"

"A name, address, work address."

"I got it. Her name is Latonya Billard, 4400 Woodbine St, Hanover, MD 21076. She works at this firm downtown called Mayco Financial. Let me know when it's done.

"I got you."

"This is time sensitive Eddie."

"I got you." He reiterated.

I left feeling satisfied with my decision, because I knew it would be completed. It was just a matter of time. Was I a coward for endangering her life and possibly my unborn baby? I was willing to do anything at this possible moment.

 I called Shawna. She didn't answer instead I leave her a message, telling her to call me because she didn't respond to my text either. I may just drop by her office, bring her lunch. She is probably wrapped up in her work. I stopped by her favorite Italian restaurant and pick up her favorite Chicken Parmesan. I continued to question myself. How did I get to this point in my life? I never in a million years thought that I would be going to these lengths to try to protect myself and my family or was I just trying to protect myself? I have to show Shawna that I'm changing. But a part of me believes I can never change.

I noticed Lisa sitting at her desk, the office looked so different. I could definitely tell that Shawna had redecorated. I asked Lisa where was Shawna's office at now. She points to the back.

"Don't tell her I am here. I want to surprise her." I whispered.

"Ok." She is smiling from ear to ear.

I was observing how things have changed. The setup and everything. I peeped through the window next to her office. My stomach began to turn. I saw her and Jamie sharing what looked like an intimate moment. He was standing behind her looking over some pictures with his hand on her waist. No wonder Shawna had seemed unfazed these days, and asking for a divorce. It looked like her and Jamie had become real close. I didn't think Jamie liked women too? I wonder how long they have been messing around. Was it before or after the cookout? I stood off to the side, and I hear Jamie mumble something as he walks towards the door. I wait for a minute then walk in on Shawna.

"Hey babe."

She jumped and it seemed like I caught her off guard.

"Hey." She says flatly. "What are you doing here?"

"I brought you lunch."

"I'm not hungry. I need to get back to work Terrance. I will talk to you when I get home."

"It looked like you and Jamie were doing more than talking about work." I say candidly.

"What is that supposed to mean, Terrance? We are not doing this right now."

"What? The fact that you're cheating too. But you all in my ass about everything that is going on?"

"Ain't nobody cheating on you Terrance. I guess you paranoid now because all of your shit done caught up to you."

"Nah, that's not what I saw."

"What did you see, Terrance? Enlighten me."

"I saw…."

Jamie interrupted, and turns his attention to Shawna completely ignoring me.

"Everything ok?"

"Yea I'm good. Terrance was just leaving."

I give Jamie a stare down, because I couldn't believe this shit. This dude just played me. My wife is playing me. I'm getting played at my own game. This was some bullshit.

"Shawna, we will talk when you get home. Here is your lunch." I dropped the bag on her desk.

Jamie

Shawna and I have become closer over the last few weeks. I would be lying if I didn't say I wasn't enjoying it. I didn't think Terrance knows I'm messing with his wife. He probably didn't even think I like women too. But Shawna is definitely a good woman that doesn't deserve what Terrance is doing to her. We have been sharing a lot of intimate moments, conversations and the sex has been amazing. I hadn't heard from Terrance in a while, but I didn't expect to either. Tonya had been calling a lot lately and I had made a mental note to call her back because she was pregnant. I needed to see what was going on with her anyway.

Terrance showed up to the office to surprise Shawna. But I guess he saw more than he wanted to according to Shawna. I could see the disdain in her eyes about everything. Apparently, she found out a few days ago that Tonya was pregnant. She popped up at her house. What the hell was Tonya thinking? She was being kind of crazy. I know I needed to move more carefully, because if Shawna found out that's my sister. Shit really is going to hit the fan. I don't know how much longer I can keep that a secret.

I was at the office a little late today. Shawna had already left for the day. I looked down at my phone and realized I had ten missed calls from Tonya. I wondered what was going on. I returned my sister phone calls.

"Hey Tonya, what's going on? Everything ok?"

"No! Everything is not ok! It's all her fault Jamie! It's all that bitch's fault!"

"What are you talking about Tonya?" She was crying hysterically.

"I lost the baby Jamie! It's her fault, I was all stressed out. All Terrance had to do was leave her. But she stressed me out too."

"Aww Tonya, don't blame anyone. Sometimes things aren't meant to be. It has to happen at the right time."

"It was the right time Jamie! Why would I get pregnant and then they take it away? That's not fair!"

"I know Tonya. But don't go and do nothing crazy. I know you're upset. I'll come over later to check on you."

"No, no I'm ok. I just need to be by myself."

"I love you sis, you take care of yourself, ok?"

"Ok."

That call was rough. I was kind of sad that she lost the baby, but on the flip side Tonya wasn't ready to be a mother. She was unstable. I knew she was probably having a hard time. Was I ready to be a step-father? If things go any further with me and Shawna, I may be on step daddy duty.

I get ready to leave the office. I looked over some last minute things. I couldn't help but to think that all of this

may catch up with me soon. How will I deal with it when
it comes?

Terrance

I get a text from Eddie a few days later.

"It's done."

I didn't ask any questions. That made me happy because I know I don't have to worry about any more outside children. But on the other hand, me and Shawna been arguing a lot lately. First over Jamie, then over other little stupid things here and there. Truth is I think she wants to leave and I don't want her to. But how do I tell her the truth about Jamie, without telling the truth about myself? Truth is Jamie and I are a lot alike except I was the married one. I didn't know he liked women too. My phone begins blaring. I looked down it was an unknown number. I answered it anyway because I did just change my number a few days ago.

"You happy?"

"Who is this?"

"You know damn well who this is!"

Aww damn, it was Tonya. How did she get my number? I cannot deal with her bullshit too.

"What do you want Tonya?"

"Well, I'm not pregnant anymore Terrance! It's all that bitch's fault!" As she continued to yell in the phone.

"How is it Shawna's fault?"

"If I wasn't so stressed about whether or not you were leaving your wife, I would still be pregnant.

"This is not her fault. Things happen for a reason Tonya."

"Oh my God! My brother just said the same thing! What is up with y'all men?"

"I gotta go Tonya."

I heard Shawna calling me through the house.

"Who were you on the phone with?"

"Work."

"Hmmm Hmmm, work?"

"Yeah ok."

Shawna don't start with this shit again."

"Whatever…. Terrance."

"You just mad because I caught you cheating on me!"

"Ain't nobody cheating on you Terrance. You see what the hell you want to see!"

"I know I saw that dude all up on you the other day in your office."

"Yeah ok, Terrance."

"I am going to mom's for a few days. I am taking TJ with me. I can't keep letting TJ see us argue like this. It's too much. I need to clear my head."

"Whatever…Shawna."

"Whatever then Terrance. I have been fighting. We still haven't been to marriage counseling. You still taking phone calls that are secrets. Tonya is still pregnant. I need some time Terrance."

"Tonya isn't still pregnant. She lost the baby. She told me yesterday." I lied.

"I knew it! You were still talking to her!"

"No, she showed up to my job!" I lied.

"Either way Terrance I still need some time to process all of this. You know where to find me if you need me."

I kissed TJ on his forehead.

"I'll see you later little man. You're just going to Grandma's for a few days ok?"

"Ok daddy. I'll see you later."

When I saw Shawna walk out the door, it made me feel like I would never see her again.

Shawna

Oh fucking well. I don't give a fuck what he thinks he saw. I was so tired of Terrance and his bullshit. Great, Tonya lost the baby. Does that make things all better? I called Jamie.

"Hey babe."

"What's going on?"

"I am about to drop TJ off at my mom's and I'll be there at your house for a few days."

"How did you manage that?"

"I told Terrance I would be at my mom's house for the next few days. He won't visit my mom because they don't like each other." He laughed.

"Ok, I'll see you soon."

After I hang up with Jamie, I called my mom.

"Hey mom."

"I'm on my way."

"Ok, honey be safe."

"Mommy, are you and daddy getting a divorce?"

I didn't directly answer TJ's question.

"Baby, why do you ask that?"

"I heard when people's parents get mad at each other a lot, they get a divorce."

"Me and daddy just need some time apart ok. You will see him in a few days."

"Ok." I'm glad TJ seemed to be satisfied with that answer.

I pulled up to my mom's house. She was so thrilled to see me and TJ. I hand her TJ's things and tell him to be good. My mom gives me a kiss on the cheek and a warm hug.

"I'll see you later mom."

I type in the GPS Jamie's address because I didn't know how to get there from my mom's house. I jumped on the highway feeling good that I get to spend the next few days with Jamie. I felt like things were finally looking up for me. I finally have a man that cares about me, and that was on my level. I grabbed my cell phone to open Pandora. I looked through my rearview and side view mirror. I saw this car speeding up behind me. I switched lanes to let them go around but they switched lanes with me. What the hell? They speed up faster. I slowed down to allow them to go around me. I get rear ended, and my car begins spinning out of control. The next thing I know I'm in the air.

I hear beeping noises; the voices are muffled…. I can barely breathe….my head hurts….I can't move…. my body feels like it has been hit by a Mack truck. I hear voices say, "we are losing her." I hear more beeping and then it begins beeping faster. I closed my eyes…. I'm too weak to fight. I tried to speak…. but my throat is dry…. I tried to scream, but I can't get the words out. What happened? As I lay here, I reflected on my life and ask myself, how did I get here? Where did I go wrong? Where did we go wrong? I had it…. I had the perfect life…. the perfect husband…. I was the perfect wife…. I had it all. I heard two voices going back and forth.

"What are you doing here?"

"What do you mean what am I doing here, what are you doing here?"

I was drifting in and out of consciousness, so I could only hear bits and pieces of the conversation.

"This is not the time nor place."

"What do you mean?"

Am I dead? People stopped talking.

Another voice enters the room. I heard her say.

"We aren't sure of her condition, and she is currently in a coma. We do not know if she will make it as the next few hours are critical. She is not alert to her surroundings. We are just waiting over the next 24 hours to reevaluate her condition."

Epilogue

I woke up drowsy. My whole body hurts. My throat was dry. I looked around the room. I recognize my husband's face. I smile weakly. I looked to my right I see another face. I wasn't sure who that was, so I just stared for a moment. Then I looked back over to Terrance. I gesture for some water. Terrance nods and pages the nurse. The nurse comes in, and says she is paging the doctor. I tried to speak. But I couldn't because all of these tubes in me. I continued to look between both men, not sure who the other was. He looked like I've seen him before, but I wasn't sure. The doctor comes in, he shines some light in my eyes, checks all my vital signs, rubs something on me feet that feels ticklish. I heard him say.

"Remove the tubes."

I gagged. It was a relief. I felt at ease.

"How do you feel Mrs. James?"

"Water."

Terrance grabs the water.

"I feel ok. My body hurts. What happened?"

"Do you remember anything that happened?"

"No, I don't." I looked confused because I wanted to know who this other man was in my room.

"You were in a very bad car accident. You have been in a coma for three days. Do you know where you were headed?"

"No, I don't."

"Do you know these two men sitting in the room?"

"Yes, that is my husband. I am not sure of this other man."

The other man spoke up.

"Shawna it's me. It's me Jamie. You don't remember?"

I look at him dumbfounded. Then I looked at Terrance.

The doctor asks, "What do you remember, Mrs. James?"

"I have a 7-year-old son name TJ. I just returned to work. As a matter of fact it was my first day back at work. I had been out of work for a while after I had my son."

He turned to Terrance. How long ago did she return to work?

"When she first returned to work was about 4 months ago."

Terrance looked worried. I was worried because he looked worried.

It appears that she may have retrograde amnesia. We wont be able to fully see until we do a MRI. Retrograde amnesia means that she doesn't remember certain events before the amnesia occurred. It may be temporary, it may be permanent. It will depend on how much damage is done to the hippocampus and temporal lobes. Right now, it's hard to say.

I get wheeled in, and I begin to get this awful headache that made me yell out in pain. I've never had pain like that in my life. I saw a flash of what appeared to be the other guy that was sitting next to me. But we were intimate. What the hell was I doing?

The doctor gets the results and rules it inconclusive saying that I would have to play the waiting game. But other than that my vitals and health looked great and that I would have to stay in the hospital for a few more days.

Terrance

I thought my heart dropped when I heard Shawna was in a car accident. Luckily, she didn't have TJ with her. I wondered where she was going? I was just happy that she was alive. I walked in and saw Jamie. We exchanged words because that was the last person I wanted to see. He was there around the clock just like I was. Did he have feelings for her? Did I deserve her? We exchanged looks then finally I said something.

"Man…you just like me. I'm just married."

"I'm nothing like you Terrance!" He said candidly.

"You into the same shit I'm into. But you up here fucking my wife."

"Yeah, I may be into the same shit. But I would never do Shawna the way you've done Shawna. That's some fucked up shit. She talked to me about all the crazy shit you've done. You just lucky she don't know you fuck men too."

"And what will she think, if she finds out you do too?"

"Whose to say that she doesn't already know?"

I got quiet. I was curious to know where she was on her way to. So I asked Jamie. I was kind of nervous to hear the answer. But I asked anyway.

"Do you know where she was on her way to?"

"Yea….. to me."

I must admit that shut me up for a minute. What if Shawna does know and is ok with it? She was going to his house. She lied to me. She must have dropped TJ off at her mom's. I guess all my insecurities are in the flesh, because if I would have dealt with my past maybe we could have talked about it. Now I stare at my wife laying in the hospital bed not sure if she is going to make it or not. I reflected on our life. She didn't deserve this. None of it.

The doctor gives us her results in which he describes as retrograde amnesia. When Shawna couldn't recall anything that had happened over the last 4 months. This is what I need. A chance to make it right, since she can't remember, it never happened. But there was possibility that her memory could return. We will deal with that when it comes.

Jamie

I was devastated when I heard Shawna had been in an accident. My mom called me to tell me that Ms. Pat's daughter had been severely injured on a highway accident. I rushed out the house and went to the hospital. The first person I saw was Terrance. We exchanged words. I shut him up. But I couldn't help but to think if I was falling in love with Shawna. Here I was sitting across the room from this man's wife, just as concerned as he was. We had the same concern in mind which was Shawna. He sat there staring at me, while I was staring at him for almost three days. I refused to leave. As much as I wanted to hate him. I couldn't help but to think how fine he was sitting across from me.

My heart sank when Shawna couldn't remember me. She didn't even remember Terrance's events. She has to remember. I just prayed that her memory would come back. Terrance didn't deserve a second chance. Terrance didn't deserve Shawna. Hell, who was I to say Terrance didn't deserve her? The way things are going I might not deserve her either. All we could do is wait, wait and hope her memory returns.

Excerpt from

Triangles of
Deception II

1

I followed her to her mom's house. I didn't want to do
anything crazy with TJ in the car. Terrance would be
devastated. I follow her. She would never know it's me. It's
all her fault that I'm not pregnant anymore. Why couldn't
she just let me have him. But noooooo she was in the way.
Where is she on her way to anyway? Well, it doesn't matter
because she won't make it there. I speed up faster behind
her, she switches lanes. I guess she thinks I'm just some
person trying to get around her. I run into the back of her as
hard as I could. I slam on brakes. I see her car spin out of
control, become airborne and flip 4 times. I hope she is
dead. I speed off. I don't know who saw me and who
didn't. I pass the accident and look over. She was definitely
unconscious. Terrance will be devastated. He will have no
choice but to come to me once he sees his wife in the
hospital or better yet dead. I hope she is dead, then I can
have Terrance all to myself. People would never
understand my plight. All I ever wanted was a good man. A
man of my own. All of these men use me, abuse me. I am a
good woman. But this particular man has made me crazy.
He gave me everything then took it away. Now I hope I
have taken away the thing that is most precious to him.
Yea, yea yea I had a mental breakdown 10 years ago in
college, no one knows but my mother, and she promised
not to tell anyone. They said I was Bipolar with
Schizoaffective Disorder, whatever the fuck that means. I
took my medication for years, up until I met Terrance. With
him in my life I felt like I didn't need them anymore. I had

been ok, stable. I would take them when I feel like I needed them. I knew when I was "off" them. But when I found out I was pregnant I flushed them all. Jamie doesn't even know. Don't judge me or my story. You have to be in my shoes to know what I'm going through. He made me crazy, yep Terrance did. I want her to suffer just like I did. You heard all the lovey dovey stuff that you think I fucked up right. Now let me tell you how things really went down. You need to know me to understand me. All Renee did was portray how crazy I was. I'm not really all that crazy, it's the men.

Q & A

1. What did you think about Terrance?

2. Do you think Shawna deserved everything Terrance has done to her even though she had her own secrets?

3. What did you think about Jamie?

4. Do you think Terrance was the reason that Tonya went crazy?

5. Did you know that Mr. Toler and Eddie were the same person?

6. Does Jamie deserve Shawna?

7. Who do you think was leaking information about the new company?

8. What did you think about Shawna?

About the Author

Renee Robinson is a first time author. She loves to read and write and has been inspired by many other African-American authors. She holds a Graduate Degree in Psychology with a background in Mental Health. This book holds near to her heart, because it will be the first time she has stepped out on faith and taken a leap at something that she has always wanted to do since she was a teenager. She has three children, all boys and married to a wonderful man. She hopes that she attracts the audience that will want to see more of her work. But this is just the beginning. If you want to contact Renee, if it's just a comment or give feedback. Her contact information is below. Triangles of Deception 2, coming soon!

Contact information:

Facebook - www.facebook.com/mzereneerobinson

IG - @mzreneerobinson

Twitter - @mzreneerobinson

Email - rnrpublishingllc@gmail.com

Website: www.authorreneerobinson.com

Mailing address: P.O. Box 25962

Richmond, VA 23260